What I condemn is the need to always defer to the science of man," Kent said.

"When our attempts to fix problems simply create a new set of problems—"

A man in another section suddenly rose to his feet. "Then we'll fix the new problems," he said. He was young but wore the braid of Starfleet commander. "It's easy to criticize in retrospect, to point out failed chains of action-reaction, but no scientist, no engineer or researcher could possibly predict every single thing that could ever go wrong. By your logic, we should all sit perfectly still, never attempt anything for fear of the consequences."

"Well, you and I both agree that there isn't any way to predict what kind of unpleasant side effects are going to rear up when you toy with nature," Kent said. "Commander . . ."

The young officer lifted his chin slightly. "Forgive me for speaking out of turn, sir. James T. Kirk."

STAR TREK®
INCEPTION

S. D. PERRY &
BRITTA DENNISON

**Based on *Star Trek*®
created by Gene Roddenberry**

POCKET BOOKS
New York   London   Toronto   Sydney

Pocket Books
A Division of Simon & Schuster, Inc.
1230 Avenue of the Americas
New York, NY 10020

This book is a work of fiction. Names, characters, places, and incidents either are products of the authors' imaginations or are used fictitiously. Any resemblance to actual events or locales or persons, living or dead, is entirely coincidental.

™, ® and © 2010 by CBS Studios Inc. STAR TREK and related marks are trademarks of CBS Studios Inc. All Rights Reserved.

This book is published by Pocket Books, a division of Simon & Schuster, Inc., under exclusive license from CBS Studios Inc.

All rights reserved, including the right to reproduce this book or portions thereof in any form whatsoever. For information, address Pocket Books Subsidiary Rights Department, 1230 Avenue of the Americas, New York, NY 10020.

First Pocket Books paperback edition February 2010

POCKET and colophon are registered trademarks of Simon & Schuster, Inc.

For information about special discounts for bulk purchases, please contact Simon & Schuster Special Sales at 1-866-506-1949 or business@simonandschuster.com.

The Simon & Schuster Speakers Bureau can bring authors to your live event. For more information or to book an event, contact the Simon & Schuster Speakers Bureau at 1-866-248-3049 or visit our website at www.simonspeakers.com.

Manufactured in the United States of America

10 9 8 7 6 5 4 3 2 1

ISBN 978-0-7434-8250-9
ISBN 978-1-4391-6924-7 (ebook)

Historian's Note

This story is set primarily in the year 2261, Old Calendar, several years before James T. Kirk took command of the *U.S.S. Enterprise*.

Love is the profoundest of secrets. Divulged,
even to the beloved, it is no longer Love.

—Henry David Thoreau

Prologue

When he woke from a restless, hollow sleep next to his wife's deathbed, Thaddeus Kent could see that she wasn't going to live much longer. It wasn't in the failing sensors that thumped and clicked over her head, though they told the story efficiently enough. It was in her face, in her *spirit,* which seemed gray and brittle, the bone-tired shadow that lay over her, sharpened her features, leached the vibrancy that he so loved in her. There would be no more weeks. No more days.

As the uncertain light of a cold morning spilled through the window, he moved closer to her, took her hand. It wasn't—it *couldn't* be—a surprise; the diagnosis had been painfully clear from the beginning. But losing her was also the most shocking, impossible thing he'd ever been forced to realize.

It will be today, he thought, watching her sleep, the lines of her face so well known to him, so loved. He made himself think it, terrified of having to face it more than once. *My Jess. Dead and gone, forever.*

He didn't think he'd cry; he'd cried too much of late. But tears formed, trickled from his hot and aching eyes, slid down his stubbled cheeks. He looked away, worked to control himself, giving up in the same instant. Maybe he was wallowing in it, and so what? Chances were very good that the next time he woke, he would be alone, all alone, his best friend stolen from him by a sickness that never should have been . . .

She made a sleepy sound, a soft inquisitive noise low in her throat. She was awake, watching him. Her fingers tightened in his, but her grip was weak, feverish.

He'd fought his own sorrow in the weeks that the disease had progressed, stealing her vitality, her life. He'd fought to be brave, not to let her see how much he was hurting . . . Because wasn't that what you did, when someone you loved was dying? Wasn't that what you were supposed to do? Put on a show of strength, help her through her own pain, let her believe that you would cope, somehow? It all seemed so foolish, now, so strangely childish. She was the only one who could possibly understand.

"I love you," he said, his voice catching. "I don't want you to leave me."

"I don't want to," she said. So quiet, so carefully medicated. She didn't have the strength to feel much of anything anymore. A blessing, perhaps. "I'm sorry."

"You have nothing to be sorry for," he said. "We were doing the right thing, you know we were."

Jess blinked, slowly. "Did we stop them?"

It wasn't the first time she'd asked, her muddled memory one of the disease's myriad complications.

"Yes," he lied, also not for the first time. He kissed her hand, held it, the sudden rage a terrible burning inside. Terrible, but so much better than the pain. "We stopped them."

She managed a hint of a smile, for which he was grateful. If she could die thinking that they'd made a difference after all, that would be something. The very least.

Jess's limp fingers twitched, an attempt to grasp his hand tighter. "Then we've won," she whispered. She met his gaze, her own bleary from exhaustion, from fighting. "You don't have to be angry anymore, Thad. It's over."

The rage was tempered by his breaking heart. She was dying because she'd cared, because she'd tried to stop a group of stupid, greedy people from ruining the small oasis that had been their home, the place where they'd grown up and where they wanted to raise children of their own. If he'd known that this would be the result, that this was even a *possibility* . . .

But what choice did we have? What else could we have done?

Thaddeus forced himself to smile for her. "That's right. It *is* over. We can rest now. Rest, my love."

She smiled back at him and closed her tired eyes. He wanted to scream, felt a million promises and regrets and plans rise into the tornado of his thoughts, the desperate need to do something, *anything,* sweeping over him like the sickness that had so effectively taken over their lives. Something had to be done to give meaning to this nightmare, to make this terrible, black day less so.

A moment later, she slipped into coma's dark embrace. Within a few short hours, she was gone.

One

Alvin Repperton was a cautious man. It showed in the careful way he held himself, the stiff posture, the constant evaluation running through his bland gaze. Even when the news he had to deliver was good—and for Carol Marcus, it was very good, indeed—Repperton didn't seem capable of relaxing into a real smile, or even a convincing fake one.

It's the funding, Carol thought, her own smile beaming back at her from the monitor's surface. *He can't convince himself that spending it is a good idea, no matter the cause.* She wondered absently if that mentality came with the job or to it, decided she didn't care. Wait 'til the team heard! They hadn't expected final word for another week.

Repperton was now referring to a data slate on his desk, scanning the information with a slight frown. Carol waited, unable to stop grinning.

"Considering your current rate of progress, we'll be expecting weekly status reports, rather than monthly," Repperton said, looking up from the padd. *"Subject to review by our staff science personnel. Standard*

observations will apply concerning material procedures. Kraden also retains the option to send a team into the field to monitor your work—or, possibly, to assist—but only if you go over the projected time period without notice of forthcoming results."

He smiled his nonsmile. *"Of course, I can't foresee any circumstance that might demand such measures. If your progress were to be so lacking, it would be just as easy to pull funding entirely."*

Carol nodded, doing her best to look properly attentive, appropriately submissive. Both her parents, university scientists, had often pointed out the necessity of being nice to the moneymen, especially when they felt the need to crack their middle-management whips. She was getting her funding, she could stand a few minutes of bowing and scraping. "Of course," she said. The message was clear enough, and typical for a private company research "grant"— get results and get them fast, or we'll stop the credit flow.

Eight weeks, she thought, and grinned again. With how well things had been going, she wouldn't need half that.

Repperton gazed at her a moment longer, his natural expression mildly sour. *"Well, then. Congratulations, Doctor Marcus. Please send notice of your receipt of funds as soon as possible."*

"I will," Carol said. "And thank you. Please thank the committee for me, as well."

"Hmm," Repperton said, a bare acknowledgment, and he was gone.

Carol stood up immediately, too excited to sit still. The small lab was empty, J.C. and Tam gone for the night, as were the handful of graduate students that came and went daily. She stepped away from her desk, paced in a circle, her thoughts racing. Tam had the list of immediate supplies they needed. They should reserve the nitrilin right away. Where would they set the final stage? Kraden Interplanetary Research had several new labs on Earth and Mars, and one or two in orbit—though Glassman was using the company's main station, she was pretty sure, and really, it would be simpler if they didn't have to transport and prep the soil. So, Mars. In spite of dome restrictions and all the current hoorah over the new land licensing, there was less red tape to get through for the type of field testing they'd be conducting; it was still frontier country out there, compared to Earth. She had to get an extended team together, ASAP. She'd already been kicking around names, mostly postgrads who were willing to work for the experience, which was best, considering the pay. They'd need a geologist, and another particle physicist, maybe one of Kessner's better "miracle" workers, if she was willing to loan one out. She wanted Dachmes for stats and mainframe prep, if she could get him; Leila Kalomi for lead on botany, assuming she hadn't already been grabbed up. And she had to call everyone, the rest of the team, her mother, Jim—

Jim. Carol stopped pacing, felt her thoughts snag. His leave was coming up, would certainly coincide with setting up a new lab. Should she tell him not to come?

No. He'll just have to be patient, that's all. I certainly have been.

That long, delicious weekend in the Cascades had been their last face-to-face, almost a month ago. He'd been busy since, getting promoted—she was actually dating a Starfleet *commander,* who'd have thought?—and was currently playing war games ("practicing tactical maneuvers," as he so charmingly corrected her) at some undisclosed location a few days away. He was due back in another ten days for the annual Federation Agenda Summit, set this year in Boston. He had three weeks of leave immediately following, and then he'd be gone again, probably for several months this time. They'd been dating only since November. Four months, and though they talked a few times a week, they'd probably spent less than two weeks together all told, most of that spread out over transporter one-nights and short weekend passes.

Knock it off. You both knew it didn't have long-term applications. Not like Inception.

Carol let it go, refusing to lose momentum. Jim would understand, he'd be happy for her, and if they weren't slated to last, she'd survive. They both would. She had a million things to do to get Inception up and running. Daydreaming about Jim Kirk could certainly wait.

Leila waited for Adam, excited and anxious as she sipped at her glass of wine, restlessly fingered the fine tablecloth. It was early for dinner, the small restaurant mostly empty. La Fresco, one of Adam's off-campus favorites. The wine she'd chosen was sweet and kind of oaky, a taste like gently decaying leaves and honey. She was on her second glass, and still she felt that low beat of anxiety, a small, heavy knot in her gut.

It's fine, she told herself. We're *fine.*

Of course they were. And he'd be pleased by her news. He'd recently commented that she needed to expand her boundaries, to start looking for something more meaningful than some prof's drudge work. Doctor Marcus's experiment would be intensive, might even mean leaving Earth for a while, but she was sure that he would approve. That he'd be proud of her.

And maybe a few weeks' absence will make his heart grow fonder, as it were. He'd been so distant lately. She tipped more wine into her glass, feeling like some character in an old movie. The nervous lover waits . . .

"Hey."

Adam sat down across from her, slightly out of breath. Leila glanced at her timepiece, saw that he was half an hour late. His pale, handsome features were the picture of apology.

"Sorry," he said, half standing to lean across the table and kiss her cheek. "Lost track of time."

"Still reworking the strings?" she asked, smiling. His thesis—a full symphonic opera—was going brilliantly, though he didn't seem to think so. He was too critical.

Adam hesitated before answering. "Right. So . . . What's the big deal? You look nice."

She sat up a bit straighter, glad she'd worn the blue dress. It was the most feminine thing she owned, light and low cut, and it was one of his favorites. She'd worn her hair down too instead of in the perpetual ponytail. "Thank you."

"Are you going to tell me, or make me guess?" he asked.

She had contemplated some clever way to slip

her news into their conversation, but now that he was here, she couldn't hold back. "I got a call from Carol Marcus today. She's been doing her postdoc at the Ell U labs. She just got funding from Kraden. And she wants me on her team."

"Really? What's she doing?" Adam poured himself a glass of wine.

"Agricultural terraforming, but accelerated. She's been working on a process that will turn nonviable regolith—ah, dirt—production-ready in a very short time. And she needs a botanist with a general agronomy background."

"Sounds interesting. Are you going to take it?" He sipped his wine, made a face.

"Yes, I think so. Whether it works out or not, I can use it as the final study for my doctorate. But I wanted to talk it over with you first."

Adam sat back in his chair. That softly irritated look she'd come to know and hate passed over his face. "Why? If you want it, you should take it."

She felt the weight in her stomach get a little heavier. "Because we're together," she said. "Because what you want matters to me."

Adam sighed. "Right," he said, but he seemed entirely unhappy with her answer.

Leila took a deep breath, decided to pursue the conversation. She'd been shying away from it for weeks, allowing her tentative inquiries to be brushed off in the hope that he would make it through whatever it was that was occupying him, but she couldn't put if off forever.

"What is it, Adam? What's bothering you?"

His smile seemed forced. "The music, that's all. Don't worry about it."

"That's what you keep telling me."

"You don't believe me?"

She swallowed, shook her head. "You've been more than distant. You say it's the symphony, but I've seen you under stress before, it's never been like this. I feel that you're angry with me about something."

At his pained expression, she reached for his hand across the table, touched his still fingers. "Just talk to me. If we can't even talk about it . . ."

She trailed off, waiting, watching. A low flush crept up his neck, across his face. He took her hand, met her gaze—and abruptly looked away.

"I think . . . I love you, Leila, you know that."

She nodded, studied his profile. Wondered if she should have kept her mouth shut.

"In the past few months, I've been thinking. With the symphony, all the time we've been apart, you always running off to do something or other for one of the profs—I've been feeling like we have less in common all the time. You know?"

She didn't respond, not sure how. The weight in her stomach was pulling her deeper into her chair.

"And"—Adam squeezed her hand, attempted eye contact again—"I . . . I think it would be best—for both of us—if we stopped being . . . exclusive."

He hurried on before she could say anything. "You need someone who shares your interests, Leila. I know you want to get married, have children. I know you want a place of your own, a stationary job—"

"You want those things, too." She was going to cry, she could feel it coming in spite of the strange numbness that was washing over her. See other people? How could he say that?

"I thought I did." He squeezed her hand once more. "I'm sorry. But I'm not ready for all that, and it's not fair to you to keep going on like this. I'm not who you want."

"Yes, you are," she said, her eyes filling. She tried to blink the tears back, failed. "If it's time that you need, I can wait. We could just . . . We could take some time. If you need to, to explore yourself with other people—" She hated the sound of it, *hated* it, but a lot of people did it, she could try. "Maybe we could arrange some-thing—"

The look on his face stopped her. Resent-ment. Guilt. Exasperation. Shame. They'd been together almost three years, and she'd never seen anything like it.

"Oh," she said, her voice small. She pulled her hand from his, that numb feeling worse than ever, her heart pounding red and loud, threatening to shake her apart. "I see."

He looked away once more, all the confirma-tion she needed.

"Who?"

"It doesn't matter," he said, his voice low and calm. "You don't know her."

Her. There it was, he'd made it real. "How long?"

"Not long. A few weeks."

Anger stirred, but weakly. She felt lost.

"What . . . what do you want to do now?" She realized as the words came out that she sounded pathetic. She should shout, throw her wine in his face, demand answers like some player in a hackneyed melodrama. Like that movie charac-ter she'd been thinking of only moments before. Strange that it didn't seem so cliché now.

"I'm sorry," he said, but he was relieved, she could hear it, see it in him. "I wasn't looking for this. But we've been growing apart for a while now, we both know it. I care very much for you, but you're so . . ." He sighed. "So focused on us. On me. You need to grow up, Lei, start taking care of yourself."

She stared at him, waiting. *This is really happening,* she told herself and couldn't fathom it.

"I can start moving my things out tomorrow," he said, his voice gentle. He reached for her hand again and Leila stood up, almost panicked at the thought of his touch now, desperate to get away, to stop listening to his horrible reasons and plans.

"Leila," he called, but not too loudly as she turned and walked away, stumbled against a table, the tears coming faster as she hurried for the door, aware that he wouldn't be coming after her.

Kent couldn't decide between the blue suit or the gray. The blue was outdated, but it fit better. The gray was newer, sharper, but he'd lost weight since the move to Mars, and it hung off his shoulders, was too loose around the waist. He didn't actually care much either way, but he had to try and look his best. The conference was always heavily covered by the media, and he needed to look the part if he meant to be taken seriously. It wouldn't do to have the leader of Redpeace looking like he'd crawled out from under a rock, the stereotypical aging tree lover going up against the youthful, respectable, well-dressed lawyers that the spoilers would likely send. Aging tree lovers got written off, and the summit could be a crucial turning point for Redpeace's aims, if they didn't blow it.

Redpeace. Kent smiled a little, aware that he too had started to think of the IF by the media's title. It was a play on Earth's legendary Greenpeace, an environmentalist group from a prior century. Six months of net frenzy and everything changed.

He gazed at the two choices another moment, then gave a mental shrug and put them both in the suit bag. He was tired; he'd decide in Boston. The rest of the packing was done, everything in order. It was still a few days until the summit, but he had contacts to meet with, and he'd be expected to help with Cady's protest gathering the day before. All that was left now was to meet the team at the office, get on the shuttle, and go.

Kent was glad not to be going alone, though he hoped that the others had paid attention to his entreaties for "improved" appearance, particularly Dupree. The wild-eyed, wild-haired environmentalist was a brilliant biologist and a truly devoted member, but she also looked like she'd been on an extended camping trip. Which, in a way, she had. Before the move, the Immutable Foundation's last project had been trying to preserve a dwindling stand of old-growth forest on Earth. Dupree had spent a considerable amount of time living in the woods, leading the defense against the developers while Kent and the lawyers had worked the zoning committee. It had been difficult and draining, particularly because the case had been so similar to the one that had meant Jessica's death . . .

Jess. Kent sat on the edge of his bed, searching for her image, finding it in his mind's eye. She was always in his thoughts, but almost twenty years had blurred everything. Sometimes he had to work at it now, to get past the memories of depression and loss, of anger and rending grief. He wanted to remember *her,* not himself.

A summer day, both of them in their late teens, an afternoon at the lake. Her dark hair, her tanned skin. Wide, lively smile. The image sharpened, became a real moment—her bare knees and feet muddy from crawling up the embankment after a swim. A smudge of drying dirt on the bridge of her nose. Both of them laughing at something she'd said, sharp and dry and so very much her, as a low sun shimmered across the water and she braided her damp hair, head tilted to one side, her fingers quick and sure. He remembered a huge feeling of love for her, big enough to scare him, thinking that if she didn't marry him, he wouldn't know what to do . . .

Maybe things would have turned out better if they hadn't married; she might have moved away, they both might have. Perhaps he would have heard the news through relatives, that their little ecocommunity was being invaded. The outrage, the need to fight might have been softened that way, might have kept both of them from caring so very much.

Pointless trying to rewrite history. The land had never really been theirs, not with the licensing laws back then. The company had been private, a group of scientists paid to find new, cost-effective ways to kill a destructive tree parasite that was eating its way through an even bigger company's profits. They'd done it, after the last appeal had gone unheeded, the last protester dragged away; their chemical/nanotech process had killed the parasites. And the ground cover. And a species of squirrel, and a half dozen species of fish . . . and Jess. The "technology" disease had been new, too. Too new for there to be a treatment.

The hospital, her strengthless fingers in mine . . .

He sighed, pushing that part of it away, the good memory going with it. He needed to be thinking of more recent efforts.

It had been hard going on Earth in the past few years. While they'd had some luck with a few wildlife habitats, they'd been unsuccessful protecting the old-growth forest, their pains mostly unnoticed, as was so often the case in these brave days of the Federation and the reckless push for continual progress by its members.

They can't ignore us anymore, though, can they? Kent stood up from the bed, felt his adrenaline give a pump. When the newly elected Martian admin announced plans to license out a healthy chunk of the southern hemisphere less than a year ago—with the Federation's assent—the IF hadn't been the only one interested. A number of public and private individuals had spoken out against the material-hungry push, citing everything from concern over the probable destruction of the Red Planet's natural beauty to anger over the privatization of lands meant for all Federation citizens. With the approval of their core members—and a temporary license from the Federation's Aid for Protected Speech—Kent had moved IF's headquarters to Mars. Within days of his arrival, the press had been all over the story, the IF had become Redpeace, and for the first time in any number of years, Kent had felt real hope. With the help of a few local environmental groups, they'd already managed injunctions against two drillers and a mining conglomerate. The people were ready; they looked at Earth and saw what could happen. The timing was right.

A push at the summit—he'd even been invited to a panel this year, a sign that what was happening was a hot topic—some real pressure on the Federation Science Council, and they would publicly condemn the Martian government's greedy agenda, might even urge sanctions. And once the FSC was on board, everything else would fall into place.

"This time, Jess," Kent said, his voice soft but certain in the quiet room. Mars could still be saved. Shoulders squared, he picked up his bags and headed out.

TWO

"Check and mate."

James Kirk stared at the queen's level a moment, then grinned, reached up, and toppled his king. The clatter was louder than he'd expected in the subdued rec room, a few people turning to look, but there was no shame in losing to Doc Evans. Doc had actually competed in the Sojkak Nationals last year and placed in the top tenth. No one aboard could beat him.

"Your game's improving," Doc said, leaning back from the table.

Kirk started gathering his hard-won pieces, setting them back in place. "Or maybe you're slipping, Doc. I hear that starts to happen, at your age."

The doctor, barely forty, laughed. "Careful, Commander. Next time, I might not go so easy on you."

Commander. Kirk felt a jolt of happiness. Though he didn't look at it, he could feel that second line of glittering braid on his sleeve, still so new. "Easy? You took me in eleven moves."

"Could've taken you in eight," Doc said. "Now then—another defeat?"

Kirk glanced up at the timepiece on the wall and shook his head. "Sorry. I've got a call to make. Thank you for the game, though."

Doc nodded, waving dismissively, already casting around for his next opponent. Kirk saw two other crewmen heading for the table before he turned and walked out; there were always takers when Doc was playing.

The halls were dim, the hour late. Kirk headed for quarters, nodding and smiling at the men and women who passed by. He recognized every face, knew every name, and was pleased that most of them smiled back readily enough, a few stopping to congratulate him on his new rank. It felt good. Since his assignment to the *U.S.S. Mizuki,* he'd gone out of his way to learn the details—who was bucking for a promotion, who was involved romantically with whom, hobbies of interest or import—and he felt it was paying off in respect and acceptance from the crew. A good first officer knew the small stuff, he thought. The *Mizuki* was *Cochrane*-class, though, crewed only 120; he wondered what it would be like to be on one of the really big ships . . .

. . . *Where you'll likely have a first officer of your*

own. Someone else to memorize the details. He grinned at his naked ambition. If and when. Besides, the captains he'd served under, those he'd respected, had made a point of knowing their men—if not the minutiae of their lives, at least the broad strokes. Captain Olin did. And Captain Garrovick always used to say—

Used to say. Kirk's smile faded as he reached the lift. It had been three years since Tycho IV, but he doubted it would ever lose its sting. If he could be half the captain, half the man that Captain Garrovick had been, he would count himself most fortunate.

The lift door hissed open and he stepped inside, putting on a polite smile for the young woman already on board. Emily Rushe, science division. Pretty. Some obscure subset of radiation physics, if he remembered correctly.

"Commander," she said at his nod. Her smile was dazzling. From their few personal interactions to date, he knew she wasn't particularly shy . . . and had expressed more than a passing interest in getting to know him better.

"Ms. Rushe."

She put on a pout, one that made the most of her full lips and arched brows, but said nothing, looking away with a small toss of her dark hair. He was being invited to play, no question.

I know better, he thought, but found himself unable to resist.

"Is something wrong?" He smiled slightly.

"I thought you were going to call me Emily," she said, turning back to him. Her expression suggested she knew she was straying into unprofessional territory, knew and didn't care.

Kirk felt a flush of wistfulness, there and gone in a second. She was awfully attractive, and he thoroughly enjoyed the company of lovely young women. But there was a fine line between flirting and looking toward a next step. He was a commander, now. He wouldn't feel comfortable pursuing an onboard romance, and certainly not with an enlisted.

Carol probably wouldn't be all that comfortable with it, either, he thought, smiling inwardly at the thought.

"I'm not on duty, Ms. Rushe, but I believe you are," he said, not unkindly. "At least for another few hours."

His tone was clear enough, and she got the message. "Yes, sir." Her shoulders straightened as she faced front. A beat later, the lift stopped and she was gone. She didn't look back.

Kirk held the control handle, shifted it, wondering if he should have managed it differently, if Emily Rushe was the type to hold a grudge.

Probably so. She was young, at least five years his junior, although so was Carol Marcus, and he couldn't imagine having to "manage" her.

It was funny, the effect that Carol had on him. From the start they'd agreed completely on keeping their options open, on not pursuing a commitment. But even with the freedom to do so, the thought of seeing other women held no real appeal. He hadn't felt so strongly about anyone since the Academy.

Days of impassioned youth, he thought, less wistful than bemused. There had been a number of women, early on, a few he'd even thought about marrying—Sharon, the lab tech he'd met through Gary Mitchell came to mind—but he'd been too young to consider it seriously, too young and too uncertain of what he wanted. And the two great loves of his final year at the Academy had been so very different. There had been Ruth, easily the most feminine woman he'd ever known, soft and warm and as delicate as a flower. And Janice, brilliant and cool, driven by ambition and intellect. He'd had serious feelings for both women, but in the end, the experiences had proved to be more about learning what he did and didn't want in a relationship than finding his soul mate.

Carol, though . . . He cut the thought short

as he arrived at his stop, reminding himself for what seemed the hundredth time that they weren't destined to be together. No matter that she was feminine and brilliant, athletic and graceful and funny—logistically, they were doomed. She wasn't Starfleet and didn't want to be, had no interest in "sailing off to who knows what," as she put it.

Doomed, he promised himself as he walked quickly to his quarters, a knot of pleasant expectation tightening in his gut. She was expecting his call. And in just a few days, she'd be in his arms, with almost three weeks of nothing but free time in front of them. They could worry about after, after.

The cool, sparse lines of his rooms were broken only by the rumpled bed and the clutter of reference disks next to his computer, topics he meant to look over before the summit. He wanted to be conversant with the big issues. To have reached commander at twenty-eight was no small feat; he didn't want to come off looking as young as . . . Well, as young as he looked.

He sat down in front of the screen, entered the appropriate codes and connectors, straightening his shirt and running a hand through his hair as he waited for the link to be established. The anticipation still got to him, even after all these months. And not for the first time, he found himself wondering if in spite of the absolute impossibility of it, she might not be the one after all. The woman he was meant to marry.

A moment later, Carol's bright and smiling face blipped on to the screen, and he forgot everything but the color of her eyes, the music of her laugh.

Leila Kalomi was the last to arrive, apologizing softly in her sweet, girlish voice before finding a seat among the other team members. She looked as tired as Carol felt, her pale skin paler than usual. Her eyes seemed bloodshot, as well, and her blond hair, longer than when Carol had last met with the botanist, was tied back in a mussed, limp tail. Carol remembered her as being much more put together . . .

. . . *And you're one to talk,* she thought, automatically tucking her own finger-brushed hair behind her ears. After staying up too late for Jim's call, she'd spent half the night going over about a hundred lists—supplies on hand, equipment left to buy, duties to delegate, what to pack. She'd slept through her alarm, something she never did, and had almost been late to her team's first meeting. The near constant high of adrenaline she'd been running on since getting the go-ahead was finally fizzling out.

My *team*. The realization gave her a boost. She smiled, stood, and walked past a stack of boxes to the front of the room. The small college lab was already half stripped, seemed bare and empty in spite of the chairs and people currently crowded into it. Most of the equipment was staying behind, it was the university's, but the accumulation of almost two years' work had taken up space, filled a lot of nooks and corners with everything from hard copy to houseplants.

She turned and faced the men and women she'd chosen, cleared her throat. The few people still talking fell silent, turned expectant faces forward.

"Good morning, and thank you for coming," she began. "I know everyone here, though I'm not sure if you all know each other. Let me start by making a few introductions."

"And who are you, again?" J.C. called out, and several of her grad student aides applauded, hooting. She grinned, shook her head.

"I'm sure everyone here knows John Carrington, for what it's worth," she said. J.C. stood and bowed, his unkempt hair flopping into his eyes. "J.C. is a molecular biologist and has been with me on this project from the start.

"Next to him is Tamara Irwin. Tam, give

a wave, would you?" The slight, dark-haired girl with owlish eyes raised one hand, her thin mouth curving into a nervous smile.

"Tam is working in particle physics and signed on about three months ago." Tam had come to the project late, a replacement for the physicist who'd laid all the groundwork, a brilliant but humorless postdoc who'd been lured away to a lab of his own. Tamara was proving to be just as capable, though she was almost violently shy, her social skills tending toward nonexistent.

Carol quickly ran through the rest of the familiar faces, the handful of grad students first, before moving on to the new.

Richard Dachmes nodded, smiling at the others as she ticked off his credentials, his projects as statistician and system programmer. She'd met him only that morning. He was a serious young man who would act as a kind of data overseer, setting up the new system and keeping the information collated; he'd also be responsible for reporting to Kraden. Although she hadn't yet worked directly with Dachmes, Carol had heard glowing reviews from several colleagues, touting his diplomatic abilities as well as his finely ordered mind, and she felt lucky to have gotten him.

There was Ben "Mac" MacCready, slightly overweight with a booming laugh, another particle physicist; not her first choice, but number one was otherwise employed, and Mac's reputation placed him at a close second. Next to Mac sat the geologist, Alison Simhbib, the youngest of the team but already published several times—her work on soil horizons in the Valles Marineris canyon of Mars, if not groundbreaking was extremely well researched, and her current interest in mineralogy made her doubly valuable. And there was Leila Kalomi, who'd already been in on any number of small experiments related to xenocrop yield.

All four of the new team members were working on their respective doctorates. There was a moment of light chitchat and hand shaking before the attention turned forward again.

"As I've already told you, the process we've been developing—which we're calling "Inception" at this point—is a fast way to make regolith production viable," Carol said. "What you don't know yet is just how fast, or how close we already are. In fact, I expect this project to be wrapped up in a matter of weeks. Possibly less than a month."

She smiled at the surprise she saw. *And they don't know the half of it, yet.*

"The heavy lifting is done," she went on. "A little fine-tuning is all that's left."

Dachmes spoke up. "So we're here because . . ."

"Because Kraden wants a proper field team to document. Considering what we're working with, they want all the *t*'s crossed and all the *i*'s dotted."

"What *are* we working with?" asked Mac.

Carol took a deep breath. "The reaction we want is triggered by nitrilin."

Mac whistled. At the blank looks from a few of the others, she quickly clarified. "Nitrilin is an extremely rare and unstable particle compound. Its only applications thus far have been military."

"Yeah, since the scientists who use it tend to blow themselves up," Mac said.

J.C. to the rescue. "Once upon a time, and they had no idea what they were working with. No one's been hurt in decades. It's dangerous only when handled improperly."

Mac was frowning. And, given what most people knew of the substance—assuming they'd ever heard of it at all—she couldn't blame him. Nitrilin had been discovered about sixty years ago, a compound of meson—quark and anti-quark—particles and a string of lepton/neutrino substructures she only barely understood herself. Its presumed discoverer, Alan Scots, had died in a lab explosion. The continuation of his work had resulted in at least a half dozen more deaths before nitrilin had been shelved by general scientific consensus. Federation Science kept it now, extremely small amounts of it suspended in antigrav fields. It was available only by application and with the strictest conditions for its use.

"I understand your concern," Carol said, "it *is* a hazardous material. But once you get a look at the work, see how we're using it, I think you'll approve. The FSC has. And it's an integral part of the Inception process. It creates a controlled reaction that vastly accelerates the infusion of appropriate elements and compounds into soil, by actually changing the atomic structure of certain molecules."

"How accelerated are we talking here, anyway?" Mac asked.

After a shy glance at Carol for approval, Tam answered. She'd been doing most of the sim runs. "Simulations are running at ten cubic acres in just under an hour."

There was a brief silence, and then everyone was talking at once. Carol grinned, imagining the stir it would cause when she published. Kraden would own the process patent, but she'd be allowed—encouraged, actually—to discuss her ideas freely in the appropriate circles, once the patent was cleared. Kraden's founders had all been scientists, certainly as wistful for fame as any lab doc she'd ever met.

"We still have a lot of work to do," she said, as the talk died down. "We're probably going to Mars, for one thing. Kraden has a new lab there, and we've got approval pending on a limited acreage study—"

"Outside?" Simhbib interrupted, her eyes bright. "Where?"

"Promethei Terra," Carol answered. "The southern highlands. The lab is self-contained—Zubrin dome—but the plot we'll be testing *is* outside. I'll need each of you to arrange for a leave of anywhere from three to six weeks. The lab has its own transporter, of course, but it's a private grade; we can't afford the energy it will use to hop out every night."

"Where would we go, anyway?" Mac said. "Aren't all the big colonies in the north?"

Simhbib answered. "Yes, but there's a small colony at Wallace. And Terra Cimmeria boasts the third or fourth largest settlement on the planet, near Kepler." Both were in easy range and would have better transport capabilities.

"Actually, we'll be relying on Federation

transporters for most of our travel," Carol said. Starfleet had shipyards on the planet, at Utopia Planitia, and in orbit. Because their labs were sometimes "rented" by Starfleet science, Kraden had preferred access to transport, or the occasional security help. "I've got a shuttle tentatively scheduled for ten days from now to take us to the shipyard station; we'll go down from there. I know it's short notice, but whatever else you've got on your plate, it can wait. My own objective opinion is that you'd be crazy to miss out on this opportunity. Now, does anyone have problems with the time line?"

Incredibly, no one did. Carol handed out the data slates she'd worked up to familiarize the new team members with Inception, basic overviews, as well as secondary units for each of the sciences involved. It was rare for any researcher to come in on a project that was so near conclusion. The slates were accepted eagerly, the excitement in the room palpable.

Leila Kalomi was the exception. She took the work with a bland smile, silent amid the bustle of interested chatter. Carol paused a moment, crouching next to Leila's chair. She saw that the skin around Leila's eyes was puffy, reddened as if from crying.

"Are you feeling well?" she asked, her voice low. "No offense, but you look tired."

Leila nodded. "I am, a little. It shows, does it?"

"I was planning to go over the material, but if you'd like to leave, I'd be happy to go over it with you later . . ."

"No, that's . . . I'm fine." Leila's smile was forced but game. "Really."

"Good," Carol said. "I'm glad you're here. I haven't seen you since . . . Since that recital your friend was conducting, remember? It's been over a year, I think."

Leila's smile faltered. "That's right. Adam's concerto. That was a long time ago."

Oh. Oh, whoops. Carol understood immediately, from the look of nostalgia and pain that fleeted across the young woman's gaze, from her tone of voice. It was a bit of a leap, but she was willing to bet that Leila's unhappy demeanor came from being recently singled. Very recently. The poor thing; she looked miserable.

She instinctively reached out, touched Leila's shoulder. "Well, you're exactly who I wanted to lead on botany," she said. "I'm thrilled you'll be with us. And I hope you and I will get a chance to catch up, later."

"Thank you," Leila said, dropping her gaze. "That would be nice."

Carol backed off and was caught up a moment later listening to Simhbib explain Martian parent rock material to Mac and Tamara.

She spent the next hour and a half going over questions and particulars with the rest of the team, pleased at the overwhelmingly positive feedback, and was relieved when Leila asked a few educated questions of her own. Whatever her personal situation, she was a good scientist, a good choice. Carol needed everyone functioning at full capacity. And she knew from her own experience that while work couldn't cure a broken heart, it certainly could distract from the pain. Perhaps Inception would prove to be as much help to Leila as she hoped Leila would be to Inception.

Pathetic. Miserable and childish and pathetic.

Leila sat on a low wooden bench in front of the Flat Garden, her thoughts as harsh and grating as the view was peaceful; the carefully raked sand and low plantings were meticulously kept. A handful of other visitors came and went, walking quietly by, pausing, moving on, their conversation low and admiring. A soft, warm breeze blew, lightly drifting through the surrounding trees, but she didn't feel it. She felt cold.

She'd been determined to get out, away from

"their" apartment, and had chosen the Japanese Gardens because they had seemed soothing the few times she'd visited before—but she was starting to doubt that anything short of a major sedative would bring her serenity. It had been nine days since he'd packed and gone, only nine, and it seemed like an eternity—tears at every turn, hours spent trying to fill her time with anything but self-reflection. She'd barely made it to the Inception meeting. And then to see the pity in Carol Marcus's eyes, to realize that she couldn't even *appear* normal.

. . . Because you're a child, isn't that what he said? That you need to "grow up." Can't even manage to look like a professional, let alone act like one. And Carol's pat on the shoulder, that kind, horrible look of understanding . . . She'd like to help, of course, a cup of tea, a friendly word; then she'll be tired of you, tired of your inability to get past this. It's not her job to take care of you. You're alone, and you may as well get used to it.

What she was starting to get used to was the near constant stream of vaguely disjointed, contemptuous thoughts, the realization of her apparent need to flounder in her own pain. The psych program she'd run on her computer had gently suggested she seek counseling for depression, brought on by trauma and aggravated by

low self-esteem. She didn't want to, couldn't
bear the thought of sharing her heartbreak with
some paid professional. So all she had to show
for her sole attempt at self-help was a new series
of abusive adjectives to add to her mental list.
Depressed. Traumatized. Low self-esteem.

Leila folded her arms across her stomach,
tight, tried to ignore the fresh tears welling up.
Her eyes ached. Her head ached. What was
wrong with her? Why did everything hurt so
much? Adam had been involved with another
woman, had kept it from her; surely she was
better off without him—

That's right, that voice of contempt broke in.
Just keep telling yourself that.

". . . And this is *Hiraniwa,* or Flat Garden."

A small tour group had approached, led by
one of the garden caretakers. In spite of her
desire not to be noticed, Leila couldn't help a
double-take. The group was entirely Vulcan,
three men and two women. They stood calmly,
quietly observing the garden as the caretaker, a
slight Eurasian man, spoke.

"It is one of Japan's earliest manifestations
of garden design," he said. "The white sand,
carefully raked into water patterns, is balanced
by the plantings of moss, grass, and evergreen.
The two shapes there, of low-growing plants,

are meant to suggest a gourd and sake cup; they connote pleasure, both spiritual and temporal. The circle of the cup signifies Buddhist enlightenment; the gourd, happiness."

The Vulcans studied the garden a moment, their faces serene. Leila surreptitiously studied them in turn. She'd seen Vulcans before, of course, but they weren't commonplace enough to ignore, not on Earth. From the curious looks the group was getting, she wasn't alone in her interest. Both women wore spare, sleeveless gowns in shades of gray and were about the same age, thirty perhaps—or so she thought. It was hard to tell. Vulcans lived longer than humans and aged very well. The men were all dressed in black, with elaborately colored shield designs on their shirtfronts. Leila had seen holocasts of Vulcan diplomats dressed similarly. One of the women spoke, her low voice lightly accented.

"The flowers are azalea, are they not?"

The caretaker smiled, nodded.

"It is similar to the *Katra-Ut-Bala,*" one of the men said. He was slightly taller than the other males, but otherwise they all seemed remarkably alike. It was the expression, or lack thereof, Leila decided. At the caretaker's inquisitive look, the tall Vulcan clarified, his voice melodic in tone.

"Garden of Living Spirit," he said.

The caretaker nodded. "I've seen holographs. The plantings used are . . . is it *favinit*?"

The Vulcan didn't smile, exactly, but his face seemed to grow more content. "That's correct. *Favinit* is planted in intersecting arcs, to represent a philosophy of oneness with self."

"There is a fine example of *Katra-Ut-Bala* at the embassy," the woman who'd spoken before added. "It has recently been opened to the public."

The caretaker bowed slightly. "I will visit it at my first opportunity. Now, would you care to see our *Seki Tei* garden, of sand and stone? I think you'll find it most interesting. In Buddhist mythology . . ."

The group moved away. Leila watched them go, feeling a pang of something like wistfulness. How cool they were, how composed. She sank lower on the bench, wiped at her eyes with the back of her hand. She felt entirely disordered, body and soul.

Certainly they *don't sit around feeling sorry for themselves,* her thought-voice supplied. No emotion to drag them down, in any area of their lives. No heartbreak, ever. Did they even experience love? Obviously not love as an emotion, but perhaps as a process, a decision, to do right by their loved ones, to work to please them, to support them. She imagined a kind of cerebral partnership, a relationship built on mutual appreciation and kindness, logic and shared interests, plans for children and a life together . . .

She cut off her mental voice before it could start telling her what she'd lost yet again, deciding that her next outing would be to the Vulcan Embassy Gardens. It was only two transporter stops from her apartment, and she could use a bit of oneness-with-self, whatever that was, exactly. At the very least, perhaps she'd be less likely to cry surrounded by a people who found it distasteful.

"Need to be more Vulcan," she murmured to herself, and at the sidelong glance from a nearby tourist couple, she stood and hurried away, adding *unbalanced* to her mental list of adjectives. It was almost enough to make her smile.

Three

The speaker, Tom Cady, wore a coverall and work boots, his long, silvering hair pulled back in a rough tail. As always, he seemed to radiate energy and enthusiasm as he spoke, pacing the makeshift stage, his words well chosen to incite. He'd already covered several of the current Earth hot points—particularly the disturbing evolutionary trends of several species of fish in the North Atlantic and the chemical spill on the African coast last winter—and was moving into some of the alleged incidents that had occurred on other worlds. An outbreak of the cold virus on Argelius II, presumably brought in on a Federation supply ship; the accidental crushing of a small colony of sand bats on Manark IV by a Starfleet shuttlecraft.

"And what is Cochrane's drive really doing to subspace?" Cady had ventured into theoretical territory. "What about the rift theory? The projection of subspace into normal space over an event horizon could cause high energy distortion waves, could conceivably destroy whole worlds . . ."

Kent, watching from the side of the stage, saw many in the crowd nodding. Cady was a good speaker. He'd been head organizer for the summit protest over the last seven years and had a long and varied history of fighting the good fight. If the small attendance—well under a thousand, by Kent's estimate, maybe half of last year's turnout—bothered him, it didn't show. Boston's early spring sun was warm and bright, the crowd comfortably spread out over the grassy lot that had been reserved for a much larger assembly. Some in the back were picnicking.

"Do I think the United Federation of Planets is evil?" Cady said, facing the eager protesters and interested locals pressed close to the platform, his voice clear and strong. "That it deliberately and cruelly seeks out new environments, new species to destroy? Of course not! We've all heard about the good that can come from what they're trying to do, the peace treaties they've helped mediate, the medicine and food they've brought to the sick and hungry. Why I'm here— why many of you are here too, I know—is because of what we *don't* know. Like what will happen to Axanar's woodlands when the UFP brings in new deforesting technology, so that every family can have their own home? Where will Berengaria VII's dragons go to breed, when Starfleet decides to mine their caverns for dilithium?

"We don't know what will happen, we don't know what Axanar, or Berengaria VII, or half a hundred other planets already have at work within their own delicate ecostructures. But perhaps the same thing will happen that happened here less than two centuries ago. I ask you, how many lives could have been saved if there had been more of Antony's Flower?"

The crowd cheered, Kent applauding along with them. It was an oft used point, but an effective one. Antony's Flower, once considered a weed in many of Earth's southern hemisphere rain forests, had proved to be a key element in the treatment of cancer. By the time Lillian Antony had discovered its medicinal properties in the last half of the twenty-first century, the plant had been all but wiped out by the heavy hand of man. It had taken years to cultivate even one-tenth of what had been lost.

"Thad."

Kent turned, saw that Don Byers had joined him. One of his core Redpeace team members, Byers looked agitated, serious beyond the content of Cady's speech. He jerked his head, motioning for Kent to come away. Still ap-

plauding, Kent backed from the platform. He
was supposed to speak, but not until Cady was
finished. Tom Cady could go on for another
hour, easily.

Byers led him through the press of watchers, toward a small group standing and sitting
near one of the park trails, just outside the rally's
boundary. There were eight or nine of them,
all young. A couple were watching the speech,
the rest talking among themselves. Something
about their casual dress, their hair, their smirking, shining faces . . . Kent slowed his pace, forcing Byers to do the same.

"Whole Earth? What's this about, Don?"
Kent asked.

Byers shook his head. "I know, I know. But I
think you should hear it yourself. Kid's name is
Josh Swanson."

Kent sighed. Redpeace, while still the IF,
had had more than enough to do with Whole
Earth, as had every other responsible environmental group in the last twenty years. Whole
Earthers advocated the preservation of natural
habitat by any means necessary. Their radical
and illegal methods ran from spiking trees to
tainting crops to wanton destruction of spoiler
equipment, and occasionally, people got hurt.
Always young, always absolutely certain of

their moral righteousness, the presence of the WE almost guaranteed bad press for accountable groups like Redpeace.

As they approached, one of the young men nodded slightly at Byers, standing to move away from the rest of the group. Josh Swanson, presumably. He was tall and good-looking, his sauntering walk a study in arrogant indifference as he wandered across their path, stopping next to an archaic drinking fountain. He had perfected the look of bored apathy.

Youth truly is wasted on the young, Kent thought, sighing again. Still, Don Byers wasn't an alarmist; if he thought it was important, it should probably be checked out. They walked to the fountain, stopping in front of the smirking young man.

"You Kent?" he asked, by way of introduction.

Byers interceded. "Josh Swanson, Thaddeus Kent."

Kent nodded at the youth, waited. Swanson smiled, an entirely charming smile that didn't quite make it to his eyes. "I've heard of you. You were in on Tyn Sei."

Tyn Sei. Wonderful. Just after Jess's death, when he'd been hardly older than the young man in front of them and nearly suicidal with rage, he and some other disaffected youth had somehow managed to blow up a chemical laboratory at an Amerasian industrial compound known as Tyn Sei, owned and operated by several companies. The lab had been a major producer of hydrazine, a hypergolic chemical rocket propellant used by Starfleet. The explosion had actually been an accident, the result of a vandalism attempt that hadn't taken into account the combustibility of hydrazine vapors, and he and the other protesters had run like frightened children from the ensuing blaze. It was easily the most foolish thing he'd ever done; that no one had been killed or even injured had been a downright miracle. And sadly, it had become the inspiring stuff of legend for groups like Whole Earth, among others. Which was undoubtedly worse than the destruction of the lab in the first place.

Again, Kent waited, neither denying nor confirming Swanson's statement. His involvement at Tyn Sei was a personal embarrassment, but it had occasionally worked in his favor. Swanson was obviously impressed, for what it was worth.

The youth studied him a moment longer, then spoke in a low, casual tone. "Kraden is about to do some experimental work on Mars.

They got their land approval, as of this morning. Fifty acres, for their lab north of Wallace."

The megaconglomerate had numerous laboratories on Earth and Mars, and was a major spoiler, a big contributor to the "progressive" Starfleet agenda. They had been lobbying for acreage in the southern highlands, but last Kent had heard, the decision was still pending.

Kent glanced at Byers. "Confirmed?"

Byers shook his head. "I put a call in to Sadler, but he's not answering."

Of course he wasn't. Since the move to Mars, Preston Sadler, Redpeace's primary lawyer, was insanely overworked. He was missing the summit this year to stay on Mars, to continue struggling with a half dozen appeals and twice that many injunctions. He was probably in court.

"What kind of testing?" Kent asked.

"Atomic-level terraform," Swanson said.

Impossible. Terraforming on Mars was strictly limited.

"Says who?" Kent asked.

"Says someone who knows," Swanson said. "Someone who's going to be there."

If it *was* true, this was big. Scientists working for Kraden had been responsible for changes, atmospheric and environmental, to a dozen Federation worlds, all for the alleged greater good of the humanoid populations living there. So far, no "lesser" species had been irreparably lost, no habitats ruined, but it was surely only a matter of time.

It had been almost 150 years since the Martian Revolution, begun over licensing issues—an Earth conglomerate had deliberately blown up sixty-five people who had refused to move off of "their" land. Native-born Martians had made the decision to govern themselves, to break free from Earth's patronage; the Fundamental Declarations had been written shortly thereafter.

And now the government wants to do it all over again, selling out to companies like Kraden. And if Kraden can get in, anyone can. The people won't stand for it, they won't!

"Thank you for this information," Kent said, as politely as he could, his thoughts racing. "It always helps to know what we're up against."

He turned to Byers, started walking back toward the rally. "Get hold of Sadler. Tell him we'll be filing for another injunction within the next twenty-four hours. In fact, you and Karen should both go back. You can help Sadler with the writing and have Karen organize a meeting with the Conservatory people, get them behind this. I've got to stay for the panel, but once the summit's over, I'll—"

"Wait, what about . . . aren't you going to *do* something?" Swanson was hurrying along behind them, the smirk finally gone from his chiseled features. He seemed incredulous, almost angry.

Kent stopped, perfectly aware of what Swanson was asking. And as impatient as he was to get things moving, he felt a reluctant responsibility to set the kid straight. After helping create the legacy of Tyn Sei, it seemed the least he could do. He nodded for Byers to go ahead before answering, keeping his voice low.

"Tyn Sei was a mistake," he said. "Anytime people can get hurt, it's a mistake. There are better ways to get things done."

Swanson looked disgusted. "Work with the system, right? I should have known. You're bought and sold, just another willing participant in the destruction."

Kent shook his head at the stock rhetoric, feeling more tired than anything else. The kid was what, twenty-two, twenty-three? The span of years, of experience, between them seemed an insurmountable barrier. What could he possibly say that would make a difference?

Try. You should at least try.

"There was a time I felt like you do, a time I was angry and frustrated with how long things take and how blind people can be," Kent said slowly. "They just break things without understanding how they work. They walk into new places and claim them as their own because they feel like they've got a right, and change them without any thought to how things ought to be. They take something beautiful, in and of itself, and decide it's ugly because it's not what *they* want."

Swanson actually seemed to be listening. He nodded, his clear green gaze angry with validation. "Right, *exactly*. Like this summit, right? The Federation says they want to honor other cultures, other worlds, and then they send Starfleet out to . . . to *violate* them."

Kent felt a rush of hope. "Yes, that's right. Their hypocrisy is shameless. And if the Martian government allows Kraden to terraform for *profit,* considering their own history, they're just as bad. It's important for those of us who care, who don't want to live in a 'progressive' reality that amounts to bland sterility and corporate comfort, to stand up and be counted, to make a difference. But when people get hurt for a cause, sometimes the cause takes the damage, you understand?"

Wonder of wonders, Swanson was still nodding. "I reach," he said, a glimmer of something like respect in his eyes. "So the thing is, if you're trying to make a difference and something goes wrong, make it look like *their* fault."

Kent stared at him a moment, his mind blanked by the perfection of the misunderstanding. As he struggled for something to say, the crowd at his back began applauding, shouting, signaling the end of Cady's speech. Kent turned, saw a few faces on the platform scanning the audience, looking for him. One of the searchers caught his gaze, beckoned him back toward the stage.

"Excuse me, I have to go." He turned his back on the youth, wondering why he'd even bothered. Whole Earth was as single-minded and cheerfully sociopathic as your typical toddler, a perpetual accident waiting to happen. Swanson raised his voice, shouted after him.

"I'll let you know if I hear anything!"

Kent waved over his shoulder without turning around, fairly certain he'd never see Josh Swanson again and not sorry for it. Redpeace would stop Kraden on Mars, through the system. And if they couldn't . . .

We will, he thought firmly, and managed a smile for the waiting crowd as he made his way back to the stage.

"Commander James T. Kirk, as I live and breathe!"

The shout was amused, almost teasing. Kirk

turned, smiling, and saw Carol walking toward him, her legs bare and tan beneath a short, casual green dress, her blond hair swept back in a loose knot. She looked as radiant as the spring day, and younger than most of the college students she moved past to reach him.

"Doctor Marcus," he replied, and stepped in to meet her. Her arms circled his neck, and he picked her up as they embraced, loving the sun-warmed smell of her hair, her light perfume of citrus soap.

She let out a slightly breathless squeal, and he set her down for a proper kiss, not caring if the whole campus watched. Just touching her had his heart hammering, and the feel of her lips on his made him ache in all sorts of ways, but he managed to step away again after a moment.

"Giving up so soon?" she asked, holding his hands, smiling up at him in that way she had, that Carol way, confident and inviting.

"Well, we wouldn't want your students to think you're not a lady." Kirk glanced around at the few dozen young people walking to or from class, or wandering across the campus lawn in small groups. A handful looked in their direction, their attention presumably drawn by his uniform. He felt conspicuous, but he was due back on the ship in a few hours and hadn't wanted to waste even a second changing clothes. From what she'd been telling him about her Inception project, she didn't have a lot of spare time, either.

"They are awfully impressionable at this age," Carol said, nodding.

"Think of the children," Kirk added, and then they were both grinning, and he felt a sudden rush of love for her that was impossible to ignore. He leaned down and kissed her again, a softer, sweeter kiss, one that promised softer, sweeter things to come. When they broke, her face was flushed, her eyes a bit glassy. He felt the same way himself.

"You learn that in Starfleet?" she asked, her voice hitching a little.

He cleared his throat, glancing around them again. "The Academy."

Still holding hands, they walked to a bench in the shade of an ancient oak tree, drawing a few more looks from passing students. Were some of those expressions less than respectful? A young couple walked by, the woman practically glaring at him. A beat later, he got a distinctly unfriendly glance from a young man with spiked, iridescent hair.

"Is it my imagination—" he began, but Carol had noticed as well.

"Probably not the best week to show up in uniform." She smiled. "There was a small rally here yesterday, to work up protestors for your summit. The big one's today, I believe, in Boston."

Kirk shook his head. "What exactly are they protesting?"

"Oh, the usual," Carol said. "Environmental causes here and there, exploitation of foreign cultures, using military as first contact, Starfleet, the Federation, and probably anything their parents agree with."

"Starfleet is extremely sensitive to the environments and cultures it encounters. Haven't they heard of the Prime Directive? And considering that some of those 'foreign' cultures consider military weakness a failing, it would be ludicrous for us to—"

"I know."

"First contact with the Klingon Empire was as friendly as we could make it, and look what happened. If Starfleet hadn't been involved, they would have—"

"Jim," she interrupted again, touching his arm. She met his gaze, her own gentle and smiling. "I know."

He made himself relax, though it took some effort. "Right," he said. "You know."

"They're kids," she said. "It's their job to protest the establishment. And Starfleet's approval rating can certainly afford it."

Deserved or not, he thought, but decided to let it go. Carol was a wicked debater, and as much as she seemed to support the Federation's goals and methods, she was always willing to argue Starfleet's handling of scientific matters. Most scientists were, he'd found. As thorough as the FSC had been, laying out guidelines for Starfleet to follow when it came to collecting and analyzing data, different specialties always favored different procedures; xenobiochemicists insisted on one way of doing things, astrophysicists another. He didn't want to argue with her, not on such a beautiful day, not when there were other, more pleasurable things they could be doing.

"That's true." He smiled. "Enough about them. How about lunch? I have to be back on the ship at sixteen hundred, but only for a half shift. After that, I'm free until the summit opens, zero eight hundred tomorrow."

"Lunch I can do," Carol said, and took his hand again. "And believe me, I'd love to see you later tonight, but I'm meeting with some of team for dinner, and it'll probably run late. Takeout in the lab."

He did his best to mask his disappointment. "Oh?"

Carol nodded, and if she was disappointed, she was hiding it well. "We got our approval this morning for the outside acreage." She grinned. "I thought we would, but there was a chance it wouldn't go through. Anyway, we'll be leaving on the twenty-third, which gives us only nine days to get ready. Can you believe it?"

"Carol, that's wonderful," he said, and meant it—but something of his feelings had to be showing, by the way she lost her smile.

"I'm sorry," she said. "I know you wanted to spend at least some of your leave with me, but we'll still have a few days. And once we get things set up at the dome, I may have some free time . . . Maybe I can arrange to meet you . . ."

"Really?" Kirk's spirits lifted. "Because the *Mizuki* is going in for two weeks at Utopia Planitia, for a panel refit. I was planning on staying here, but if you think you'll have time, I could stay with the ship . . ."

"I will," she said.

"I don't want to impose," he said, which was as close to a lie as he'd ever told her. He wouldn't have another extended leave for six months, at least, and had planned to spend *all* of

his R & R with Carol. "It's your first project as
director. You'll be busy and probably won't be
in the mood for candlelit dinners and long walks
in the starlight—"

Carol leaned in and touched his face, ran a
finger across his lips to still them.

"I'll be in the mood for *you*. We'll make time.
After all, who knows when we'll meet again?"

She said it lightly, but both their smiles faded
after a beat. They generally avoided talking
about the future, but there it was—he was career Starfleet, looking toward a command of his
own, and she wanted to put down roots, run her
own lab. There was no future.

Carol stood up, breaking the awkward moment. "So, I know this great place just off campus. There's wine, cheese, coffee . . . leftover
barbecue too, I'm pretty sure. If not, we can always order in."

She gave him that particular Carol smile
again, coaxing him to his suddenly somewhat
shaky legs as he realized the very place she
meant.

"There may not be much of a menu, but the
desserts are excellent," she said, her voice low,
that smile telling all.

"Sounds perfect." They started away, Kirk
wondering how he'd gotten so very lucky,

wondering if perhaps the lack of future need necessarily be set in stone.

Lieutenant Commander Spock stood at the edge of the *Katra-Ut-Bala,* studying the rows of plantings in their gentle, ancient design. The attractive garden arrangement, a representation of the many facets of self-achieving oneness, dated back to Surak's time. Spock appreciated the historical component, as well as the philosophical symbolism of many becoming one. It appealed to him in a way that some of the other embassy exhibits did not. The painted depictions of the Voroth Sea, for example, struck him as overly colorful, not at all like his own memories of that body of water. He recalled it as stark and monochrome. Of course, he had been a child then, and his visit to the sea had been for only a few days; perhaps a change in season wrought changes with the light of which he was unaware. Or perhaps the artist's perception was simply unlike his own. Art was an entirely subjective field, after all.

Spock moved toward one of the flat stone benches that flanked the garden. He had no reason to hurry, and the day was mild, cool but not overly so for this time of year on Earth. He would sit, observe the garden, reflect on the artistry of the gardener. A human, one George Iles, had long ago stated that art was "a handicraft in flower," a poetic sentiment but one that seemed appropriate to the particulars of ornamental gardens.

A young human woman was sitting on the bench next to the one he'd chosen. She too seemed quite taken with the *Katra-Ut-Bala,* or so he might assume, if he were one to do so; she'd been at the garden when he had arrived. At the moment, they were the only two visitors. As he sat, she smiled at him, nodding her head pleasantly. He nodded in turn, then resumed his study.

After a few moments, the young female stood and stepped over to his bench. "Excuse me. I'm very sorry to bother you, but may I ask a question?"

Spock looked up. The woman wore an expression of apology, a frown, a hesitant smile. Her hair was a very light blond, her face pale and evenly featured. He was uncertain as to how to respond to her opening statement, but her query was simple enough. "You may."

She sat next to him. "Is there some significance to the number of rows, do you know?" She looked back at the garden. "I ask because I noticed that there were also seventeen rocks in a line across the *Kir-Bala*."

She referred to the Garden of Perception, on the other side of the embassy. Spock had visited it often.

"It's a reference in Vulcan mythology," he said.

She nodded, apparently expecting more. Ever mindful of his position as an ambassador—for all Vulcans on Earth were that—he accommodated.

"Traditional fiction tells that there were seventeen paths to the *Pa Ut'ra,* a fabled monastery. Literally, Place of Insight. The number is common in Vulcan art, particularly with themes of self-awareness."

"Was there such a place?" she asked. "A basis for the myth?"

"Unknown," he said. "Definitive research is not possible."

"Why's that?"

"The myth is several thousands of years old and suggested that *Pa Ut'ra* was in a place that no longer exists. On a mountain, in fact, where there is now a vast desert. There would no longer be any empirical evidence to uncover, if there ever was.

"There is a kiosk inside the embassy that offers a historical overview of Vulcan, if you wish to pursue the topic in more depth," he continued. "Reference cultural mythology, prior to the Time of Awakening."

She smiled again, again that hesitant, faltering smile. "Oh. Thank you."

There was silence between them, but the human girl stayed seated. She looked at him, then away, then opened her mouth as if to speak again, and closed it. Although Spock didn't generally find emotion easy to read, her actions strongly suggested indecisiveness.

"You have another question?" he asked.

She smiled. "I have a lot of questions, actually. I'm sorry, am I keeping you . . . ?"

Spock briefly considered her statement and its implications. She wished to speak further and was exhibiting apology for the intrusion on his time. If he chose not to converse, the appropriate response would be for him to explain that he was, in fact, occupied. If he was willing to undergo additional questioning, he should—

"I'm bothering you." She stood. "Excuse me, please. And thank you for your time."

"I am not bothered," Spock said, aware that he had hesitated for too long. In spite of the fact that the majority of his interactions had been with humans for 13.62 years, he had yet to master any of the subtleties of "casual" conversation.

Including, it seemed, the need to respond in a timely fashion.

The woman continued to stand but was smiling again. "Well, I'm glad to hear that," she said. She had a slight accent that he had not heard before, a certain crispness to her words, though her voice was light, mellisonant in tone. "I didn't come here to bother anyone."

"As is expected," he responded, determined to hold his end of their interaction but not sure what else to say. Why would anyone travel to the Embassy Gardens in order to harry visitors? As had been pointed out to him in other instances, he was, perhaps, taking the statement too literally.

She laughed, a soft sound. "My name is Leila Kalomi," she said, sitting again.

"I am Spock." He considered stating his rank and post, but that seemed overly formal under the circumstances.

"I'm pleased to meet you, Mister Spock. I'm very curious about the gardens here. And you're the first person I've had the courage to talk with all day. I'm a bit shy, I suppose."

She looked down and away. "If you have other plans, I wouldn't . . . I mean, if you're not too busy, would you mind walking with me through a few of the exhibitions?"

Her manner—expression, words, the "shrug"—was self-deprecating, Spock decided. She approached their interaction as though afraid to approach, as though unworthy of his consideration, yet if she truly believed that to be so, why had she approached? It was illogical but representative of an interesting duality he'd noted before in his interactions with humans, particularly in social dealings—the expression of regret for daring to discourse. He had theorized that his Vulcan ancestry was the cause. For as many racial slights as he'd experienced among humans—not nearly so many as he'd endured throughout his childhood on Vulcan—he'd also encountered those who seemed to feel concern that their own ancestry might somehow be an affront to his. They could not know that his heritage was mixed, of course, as this young woman would not. But by her own admission, she had been reluctant to speak to *another*. Considering the environment, it was probable that she meant another Vulcan, which lent credence to his hypothesis.

Aware that she was waiting for his response, he put the thoughts aside, refocusing on the more immediate. In fact, he had nothing to do that could not be postponed. His plans for the day had included the gardens, a meal—there were a number of fine vegetarian restaurants near the embassy—and perhaps a visit to a museum of science and industry, this one in Paris. He'd seen four such museums over the past six days, had been visiting them by number of points of interest. The Parisian museum allegedly had an excellent film archive, historical documentation of Earth's first industrial revolution, as well as several working mechanical specimens from the era, including a loom and a number of steam-driven engines. Earth history was a current hobby of his, one he'd been extrinsically motivated to indulge; had he been given a choice, he would be aboard the *Enterprise,* overseeing the Starfleet Corps of Engineers' modifications to the warp drive. The starship was in dock for another month, after which it would return again under Captain Pike. But after he had learned that Spock meant to remain aboard throughout the ship's lengthy reconditioning, the captain had ordered him to stay away for "at least" two weeks. And since he was not planning to attend the Starfleet summit, that left eight days—minimum—to fill with seeing "the sights," as the captain suggested.

The woman had expressed interest, and as his homeworld's mythology was quite intricate, and a subject in which he felt himself conversant, it seemed logical that he should tour the gardens with her. He had visited them every day of his exile and knew them well.

"I would not mind," he said, and the brilliance of her smile, the look of happiness that crossed her face, pleased him more than he would ever admit, even to himself.

Four

Carol waited for the courier, Mac and Tam at her side. The university's bland transporter room was empty except for the two techs standing at the control console, talking in low tones about some recent sporting event. Both physicists were silent, Tam's aversion to conversation having finally thwarted Mac's numerous attempts to get one started. The gregarious MacCready had already tried with Carol, but she was too preoccupied to muster much of a response. She was tired, scattered, and something she'd eaten for breakfast was definitely not agreeing with her stomach; too much coffee, perhaps. In all, it wasn't shaping up to be much of a day. Yesterday had been better.

Waking up to Repperton's message should have clued me in, she thought, resting one hand on her uneasy gut. *Should have just gone back to bed.*

Wishful thinking. With the project so close to completion, she couldn't afford the luxury of sleeping in.

Or sleeping, she thought, remembering her

extended lunch break from the day before. She smiled slightly, wistfully. Jim would be in Boston for the next several days, the duration of the summit. While it would be easy enough for them to continue meeting, they had agreed it would be best for both of them to keep focus on their respective tasks. As important as Inception was for her, the summit was an opportunity for him, one he'd spent weeks preparing for. When it was over, they would work something out for the remainder of his leave.

Midnight trysts on Mars, I suppose. Another smile. *Kisses stolen beneath a salmon sky.* His presence on Mars would definitely be a distraction, but one she thought she could manage. *Would* manage. She wasn't sure if she loved him, not yet, but she was leaning in that direction. And he'd made his own feelings clear. He could be so direct sometimes, so absolutely certain, it was a little frightening.

He said it, she thought, and felt her heart thump an extra beat. *Looking into my eyes, no banter, no apology. No question. Simple as that.*

It wasn't simple, though. She didn't want a long-distance relationship and didn't think that he did, either. But she also couldn't imagine breaking things off. She had spent all of her young adult life knowing that if it came down to romance versus career, career would win. And now that she was actually faced with such a choice, all she could think about was his clear, direct gaze, when they'd finished making love, the complete resolution in his voice when he'd told her that he loved her.

Her stomach twisted a bit, dragging her back to real time, reminding her of that extra cup of coffee and the reason she was standing around, wasting precious time. She was about to ask one of the techs to call the departure point when he spoke into his console, adjusted a few switches. He nodded to the other tech—a student, apparently—explaining what he was doing as he worked the controls. The high, rising whine of the transporter drowned out their soft conversation.

"Nice of them to be on time," Mac grumbled. Carol silently agreed.

Two men shimmered into view, one wearing a Starfleet sciences uniform, the other, much younger, in a business suit. Carol smiled mechanically at them, barely able to pull her gaze from the lock case at their feet. The science officer picked it up, stepping off the pad, a look of polite apology on his face. The young man in the business suit followed, his expression blank.

"Doctor Marcus?" the science officer asked, and Carol reached in, shook his hand.

"Aaron Thiel," he said. "Sorry for the delay. We had . . . actually, there was a processing problem at—"

"It was my fault," the other man interrupted, smiling a practiced, artificial, entirely unapologetic smile. He looked like a teenager. "The FSC didn't have the forms correctly filled out, I had to insist that we get all the proper authorization codes."

He reached for Carol's hand, held it limply. "The Council is trustworthy, of course, but you let something like that slide, before you know it, no one wants to do the work. I'm Troy Verne. Repperton said he would remind you I was coming. He didn't forget, did he?"

He held her hand a beat too long. Carol pulled hers away, hoping her own smile seemed more sincere. "No, he left me a message this morning. Although I hadn't been informed prior to this that Kraden would be sending a . . . representative."

"What, you thought they'd let you work with something like nitrilin without covering all bets?" Verne chuckled. "Not going to happen. Where the nitrilin goes, I go. In this case, off to Mars, to watch you folks play with somebody else's ecosystem. Lucky me, right?"

Was he trying to be insulting? *Keep smiling.* "I
assure you, Mister Verne, that we're not 'playing' with anything here," Carol said as evenly
as possible. "If we're successful, our work may
help alleviate famine throughout the galaxy,
perhaps even prevent tragedies like Tarsus IV.
The FSC has approved and endorsed our pro-
posal, and we plan to be very, very careful."

"Right, of course," Verne muttered, in a
tone that suggested he was dealing with a mad-
woman. "I'm sure. I'm just here to . . . Technically, you're an independent contractor for
Kraden—not a direct employee—and they want
to be certain that there are no misunderstandings. You know, in the very unlikely event that
there are any, ah . . . misunderstandings."

*So that if we blow up Mars, Kraden can say it's
our fault, not theirs.* She should have expected as
much, but hearing it fumbled out by this arrogant young man was almost more than she
could take.

She hung grimly on to her smile, introducing Mac and Tam to both men. When Mac
asked Verne if he was a scientist, Verne actually
laughed, explaining that his specialty was "management" but that his background was in law.
It seemed he had an aunt on Kraden's board of
directors, and had just started his new job there,

that this, in fact, was his very first project. Carol smiled until her teeth were dry and thanked her stars that Mac was so friendly, the physicist asking Verne any number of blandly pleasant questions while she conferred with Thiel.

Finally Thiel had her sign a data slate and print it, then handed the locked case to her, along with a key strip. He shot a distinctly sympathetic look at her, rolling his eyes toward Verne, and then was gone, leaving them with Kraden's rep. Their new lab mascot, it seemed.

At least they could have sent a scientist, Carol thought, as the four of them started for the lab, Verne trying to engage the two physicists in a conversation about terraforming laws on Mars. It was hard to tell whether or not he approved of their experiment; he wasn't unfriendly, exactly, but he made another offhand comment about them "playing" with habitats, as though he wanted to alienate the trio of scientists. Whoever his aunt was, she must have pulled more than a few strings. Either that, or Kraden thought so little of the project, they didn't care whom they sent. Carol preferred the nepotism angle.

Mac kept his game face on, but Tam looked miserable, already completely scared back into her shell by Verne's insistent attention. Carol would have to take him aside at some point—

soon—and try to explain a few of the intricacies of living in a small, highly focused project group.

My *project group,* she thought, and as Verne prattled on, proclaiming his rapture at being a "team player," she felt another sudden, unhappy lurch of her stomach and decided that she definitely should have stayed in bed.

The first open-to-all panel—a reveal of the projected time line for Federation expansion over the next decade, as well as specific missions setting out in the upcoming year—wasn't scheduled until early afternoon. The morning of the summit's first day, it seemed, was devoted to chaos. Arriving Starfleet personnel milled about in the lobby of Boston's Federation Assembly Hall, mixing with Federation ambassadors, representatives from a dozen worlds seeking membership, grand administrators and lower-echelon management from around the galaxy. Captain Olin had already introduced Kirk to an endless parade of unfamiliar faces, finally excusing himself to talk shop with someone or other, leaving him to fend for himself.

Kirk stood near the lobby's far wall, looking over his agenda slate as people swarmed past, the handful of musical languages being translated simultaneously creating a low roar. There were lists of visiting ambassadors, timetables for panels open and closed, short treatises on everything from possible general order amendments to recommendations for SCE projects. It was his first Federation summit, and while Kirk wanted to make the most of it, make connections, he felt a little overwhelmed. He'd gotten used to a closed environment.

"Jim? Jim Kirk?"

Kirk looked up, startled to see a somewhat familiar face, one he hadn't seen in a long time; it took him a moment. The man wasn't much older than himself, wore civvies, had light hair and a beaming grin. An attractive young blonde stood at his side, the similarities in their facial structure suggesting that they were related.

"Paul Marshall," the man offered, just as it occurred to Kirk. Marshall had been one of the science cadets on the *U.S.S. Republic,* from the Academy days. He was usually better with names, but seeing Marshall out of uniform had thrown him.

"Paul," Kirk said warmly, shaking hands. "I didn't recognize you, keeping company with someone so attractive."

The blond woman smiled, and Marshall threw one arm around her shoulders, mock-growling at Kirk. "Watch it, *Commander*. That's my sister you're talking about."

"Janet Marshall," she said, shrugging off her brother's arm. "Nice to meet you."

"Jim Kirk, and he's not someone you want to have anything to do with," Marshall said. "Not unless you want to take a place in line. Jim had about a dozen girlfriends back at the Academy, if I remember right. And half the gals on the *Republic*."

Kirk rolled his eyes as he shook hands with Janet. "Your brother has a talent for exaggeration."

"And you've got one for understatement," Janet replied. Her smile was lovely, her voice soft and very feminine. "According to Paul, every man in Starfleet is a raging lothario. Or at least every one he's introduced me to this morning."

"Perhaps meeting you is an inspiration," Kirk said, and Janet laughed.

"Enough already," Marshall said. "Jan, you're going to be late . . ."

"Right. It's been a pleasure, Commander." She turned to her brother. "Paul, I'll see you this evening?"

Marshall nodded, and with a final smile and wave, the young Miss Marshall disappeared into the crowd.

"She's an intern with the FSC," Marshall said. He was obviously proud. "Studying endocrinology. Though she'll probably end up in the private sector rather than Starfleet. Less backing but more freedom."

"Is that where you are?" Kirk asked. He remembered that Marshall had been a research chemist of some sort.

"Yep. Good thing, too. If I'd stayed in, I'd have ended up having to call *you* sir."

Kirk laughed. The two men chatted amiably a moment, catching up on shared acquaintances, on personal achievements. Marshall was head of R & D for a company that manufactured pharmaceuticals and was attending the summit in a professional capacity. The company he worked for had a contract with Starfleet.

"Head of your division," Kirk said. "Impressive."

"Thank you. I don't know if it has anything on making commander, though. You're on the fast track, Jim."

Kirk shrugged, pleased in spite of himself.

"You want to see something *really* impressive?" Marshall asked.

He pulled a small flat object from a pocket, held it out. Kirk took it. It was a capture print, a smiling woman with red hair holding a grinning baby, the child perhaps six months old.

"Marie and Paul Junior," Marshall said.

"Beautiful." Kirk studied the picture a moment longer, the woman's kind eyes, the baby's chubby fists in his lap, then handed it back. "Really, a beautiful family."

"Something else I couldn't have done, if I'd stayed in."

"People in Starfleet don't have families?" Kirk smiled.

"Do you?" Marshall asked. When Kirk hesitated, Marshall nodded, his expression knowing.

"Not yet," Kirk protested. "Someday."

Marshall's look said volumes. Kirk shrugged again, inwardly this time. To each his own.

"Like I said," Marshall said. "Anyway. I've got to get back to the hotel, do some research for my afternoon meeting. Walk me out to the pads, if you don't have anything better to do."

Marshall nodded at Kirk's uniform, smirking. "Maybe you can incite the protestors."

Kirk walked with him toward the lobby doors. "They're here?" he asked. "I thought their support rally was yesterday."

"It was, but you think they're going to pass up the extra coverage?"

Kirk barely heard him as they stepped outside and were confronted by a sea of activity that made the summit chaos seem almost orderly.

So many, Kirk thought, studying the yelling crowd that pressed against the low-grade force barrier that lined the walk to the transporter pads. There were a few hundred of them, at least, most dressed in garish, youthful fashions, talking, singing, many holding signs or flags that spoke for them. Some of the signs were quite sophisticated, animated holopic images and professional logos; others merely looped through two or three generic antiestablishment phrases, repeated in multiple languages. The protestors nearest the lobby doors held their signs toward Marshall and Kirk, shouting. A group of young people who wore nothing but body paint and strategically placed flowers shook their fists at Kirk, one of them demanding that Starfleet "let evolution become." Two of them carried guitars, another wore a drum around her neck.

"Does anyone take these people seriously?" Kirk asked.

Marshall shrugged. "Some of them have been invited to run counterpoint this year, on the summit's last day. An open panel. Called 'The Cost of Expansion,' something like that."

"Which ones?" As they started for the nearest transport site, Kirk had to raise his voice to be heard. "The naked teenagers? Are they going to debate, or sing a song?"

Marshall laughed, but Kirk wasn't sure it was funny. He knew that there were environmentalist groups with legitimate concerns, but there were also whole branches of Federation science and admin designated to address such matters. What had gathered outside the summit was a much more radical element. Kirk was surprised that the organizers were granting them recognition of any kind.

One of the animated banners caught Kirk's eye—the image of a beautiful, shining red marble of a planet—Mars, obviously—that faded, turned gray and dead, and finally burst into flame. Kirk frowned, annoyed by the obvious extremism. One of those gathered beneath the sign, a tall, lanky man in a blue suit, appeared to be in charge; he was speaking to a handful of netcams, his expression serious. As he and Marshall walked past the interview, Kirk caught some of what the man was saying.

". . . But it's not just about advancement versus apathy, moving forward or growing stagnant, as a culture. There are bigger issues here, questions about *how* we want to progress, and what it means to be progressive . . ."

The man's tone was as reasonable as his

words; Kirk had to resist an urge to stop and listen. It seemed there was a semilegitimate group out there, after all, or at least one that wasn't outright mad. But if their sign was representative of their reasoning, that made them far more dangerous than a thousand painted children.

The man in the blue suit locked gazes with Kirk, just for a beat. Kirk stared back at him, seeing intelligence, purpose, and . . . anger. As though Kirk was personally responsible for whatever slight had brought him here, to stand outside a meeting place of sane and reasonable men, to ally himself with a carnival of disaffected youth and idealists grown bitter.

I see you, Kirk thought, and nodded, so slightly that it was perhaps imperceptible. Whether the man saw it, he couldn't say. He continued speaking, and in another beat, was out of sight.

"Miss Kalomi?"

Leila looked up from the data slate she was reading, both startled and pleased that Mister Spock had found her. They'd made no plans to meet, but during yesterday's interesting and informative walk, he'd said that he had visited the gardens every day of his leave thus far, and she'd hoped very much to see him again. It seemed that her lingering lunch by the entrance to the gardens had been well timed.

She set the slate aside, cleared away the remnants of her lunch so that he could sit next to her. As before, he was in uniform, and it occurred to her that she'd never seen another Vulcan wearing Starfleet. It suited him.

"*Malus domestica,*" he said, sitting, his voice without inflection.

She picked up one of the two remaining apples from her meal, nodding, unable to keep herself from smiling. She had brought them to eat, not as a conversation topic, but she found herself pleased that he knew the genus.

"Yes, but these are a little more than that." She held up the small fruit. "They're cross-pollinated with a fruit native to Ta'utre VII that has a much slower rate of decay." A colleague of hers had worked on the grafted strain as part of her graduate thesis project, a fast-growing, high-yield variety that kept incredibly well. Leila had helped with the research, assisted with some of the fieldwork, and had been "paid" in apples, bushels of them. The apple she held was from one of the original crops, picked nearly a year before, but she knew it would taste as though it had just been harvested. She and Adam had gone through seeming thousands of the things . . .

She swallowed that thought, looked up into Mister Spock's intent gaze. He seemed entirely focused on her, on what she was saying, as he seemed to be every time she spoke. A Vulcan trait, presumably, one that she found . . . flattering, in a way. As though he really wanted to hear each word.

"Was that grown on Ta'utre VII?" Spock asked. "It would explain the small size. Ta'utre VII's gravity is slightly higher than that of Earth's. Point oh-eight six, to be precise."

"Yes, that's right," she said. "The trees are much smaller and straighter than the Earth variety, the branches more compact, but the yield is actually higher. And the fruit reaches maturity in about an eighth of the time. Also, these apples were cultivated specifically to be less acidic than any Earth variety, so they won't trouble the stomach. Even the seeds are edible."

Spock continued to study her, his gaze inscrutable. Leila realized that she was still holding the apple up and suddenly felt foolish. She lowered her hand. It was difficult to explain the excitement she felt talking about her field, the personal satisfaction. Adam had often teased her about it.

"Forgive me," she said, smiling. "I tend to

talk too much about things that would only be of interest to another botanist."

"As I stated before, botany is an interest of mine," Spock said.

"You did," Leila said. He probably thought her hopelessly emotional, but he was so straightforward, so direct, that she couldn't help smiling. "I probably enjoy talking about it a little too much, though."

Spock's chin lifted very slightly, and he blinked. "I believe it is only logical to take pride in the products of one's study."

She thought she detected a kindness in his gravelly voice, but perhaps she only wished it so. Was pride an emotion?

"Would you like to try one, Mister Spock?" she offered.

"Thank you." As he took the fruit, his fingertips brushed against her palm, his skin cool against hers.

He took a bite, swallowed.

"I detect a particularly high concentration of fructose in this specimen," he said. "But somewhat less pectin than one might expect."

"That's right," she said. "It's sweeter than most Earth varieties. Not too sweet, though. I mean, I hope not overwhelmingly so."

"It is not. It is quite pleasant."

Leila took a bite from the last apple, to hide another smile. She'd heard that Vulcans couldn't lie, or didn't, she wasn't sure which, but it was a trait she could certainly come to appreciate. He was so honest, even his small acknowledgment of the apple's taste was like a grand compliment.

They ate the fruit in silence, Leila enjoying the quiet, the soft sunlight, the company. Was Spock enjoying himself? She hoped so. He'd joined her, hadn't he? Perhaps he was only being polite, but she didn't think so. No, he could have said hello and gone on about his business. He'd stopped to sit with her because . . . because perhaps he was lonely, too. Vulcans didn't express emotion, of course, but they *were* social creatures; they lived together, worked together. She knew she might be projecting a bit, but he'd told her that his captain had ordered him to leave his ship, to find something to do, and he'd obviously been at loose ends, visiting the Embassy Gardens every day.

And he told *me he would be here,* she thought, finishing her apple. *If he wished to avoid me, he need not have said anything.*

"Efficient food production is the nature of your research?" he asked.

"Holistically, I'd say yes, but my true focus is much narrower, concentrated more specifically on soil structure," she replied. "The project I've just started working on involves altering the ratio of microorganisms to enzymes in Martian regolith. But if everything goes well, the applications will be practically universal."

The Vulcan's curiosity was clearly piqued. His head cocked and his dark, piercing eyes narrowed. "Applications?"

Leila nodded. "High-production agronomy using previously nonviable regolith." She indicated the data slate on the bench next to her. "I'm still learning about it myself."

"There are numerous studies concerning regolith terraformation for agronomous purposes," Spock said. "An interesting field."

"Yes, but this project will be groundbreaking," she said, smiling at the play on words. Spock did not.

"In what way?"

"The team I'm working with has found a way to alter regolith chemical composition in a matter of hours, rather than months or years. Using nitrilin as a trigger."

Spock frowned. Leila wondered if Vulcans were capable of surprise, decided that they had to be. A reaction wasn't an emotion, was it?

"A volatile substance," Spock said. "I was not aware that it had applications to terraformation."

"I wasn't either, but the data is sound." She again nodded at the slate. "And they . . . we've already received approval from the science council. And acreage on Mars for the fieldwork. We'll be leaving Earth in just over a week."

"Fascinating," Spock said. "Might I access copies of this data?"

Leila hesitated. It would be unprofessional for her to leak project information to another scientist, or at least anyone not working for Kraden. But Doctor Marcus hadn't specifically asked that they keep the data under wraps. Not from friends and family, anyway. Spock wasn't exactly her friend, but . . . but she could trust him. She felt sure of it.

"Most of it hasn't been published yet, it's all based on recent research," she said. "But it's not restricted material. You should be able to access most of the relevant documents from the university mainframe, though you have to be a student or faculty to get to it. I could do a retinal scan for you on your computer, if you like."

"I do not currently have access to my personal computer," Spock said.

Of course not, his was on his ship. Leila hesitated again. She couldn't just copy off the slate, the data was encrypted against it, and she needed to keep her own copy of the exact specs . . .

. . . But I could download it, she thought. *Access and copy the appropriate university files . . .*

"My apartment is nearby," she said, her heart speeding up a few beats as she said it. Had she just invited him to her apartment? To her and *Adam's* apartment? The place was in a terrible state of disarray, he was still hauling his things out, to move in with *her,* presumably . . .

She forced that thought, those regrets, into a secure package, to be reopened at another time. She was being ridiculous. A Vulcan wouldn't care about something as irrelevant as a messy apartment; neither should she.

"We can use my computer," she added and stood up. "It shouldn't take long."

Spock gave a quick bow of his head, presumably in agreement. Aware that she was blushing a little, Leila quickly rose and started for the embassy transporters. Spock followed her without a word.

Five

Leila Kalomi scanned a triadium card, about five centimeters square, in front of a tiny panel beneath the door lever. Spock noted that the security system on her living unit was quite rudimentary. The key card would be simple enough to duplicate, could certainly be formulated in a very basic laboratory environment.

"I'm sorry for the mess you're about to see," she said, pushing down the door lever.

"There is no need for apology," Spock said. Organizing one's possessions reflective of *memsha'rup* was a Vulcan tradition. It was logical to expect some degree of chaos in a dwelling inhabited by humans.

Miss Kalomi roughly wiggled the door. The automatic rollers seemed to be jammed. Spock hypothesized that the air-controlled caliper was malfunctioning, had seized in an open position, perhaps as a result of oxidation, or, possibly, an accumulation of matter over time. The building was quite old and didn't appear to be particularly well maintained. The caliper would need to be removed and cleaned, possibly replaced entirely. He grasped the door just above the young lady's head and pushed it back.

"Thank you," she said. She seemed out of breath; strange, as her struggle with the door had not been prolonged, and she appeared to be in good physical condition. Appropriate to a human female, certainly.

"You are welcome," Spock said.

They moved inside, and Spock assessed the small apartment. Nearly every surface in the room they had entered was piled high with objects—boxes, cases, articles of clothing and old-fashioned books. The apartment appeared to be in the midst of some kind of transition.

"It's a wreck," Miss Kalomi said, her face suddenly changing color. Spock noted the physiological change, interested; she seemed prone to such flushes. He understood that visible dermis changes of this sort suggested strong emotion in humans—as in several other humanoid species—but could not imagine why Miss Kalomi would currently be experiencing such a change. Anger? Embarrassment? If she had been unaware that her apartment would be in such a state, it could be surmised that someone else was responsible for it—an intruder? Possible, considering the lack of sufficient security in the building. But Miss Kalomi was not exhibiting any of the traits he would have associated with fear in a human, and she *had* apologized for the disarray before they had entered the dwelling, which made anger—or, at least, anger borne of surprise—seem unlikely.

Miss Kalomi hastily gathered a few items of clothing from a chair, setting them aside before moving toward a cluttered computer console. "Please sit down, Mister Spock."

He did so, his attention drawn to a shining musical instrument in an open case near his feet. He recognized it.

"A French horn. Does this instrument belong to you, Miss Kalomi?"

The color in her face seemed to intensify, and Spock briefly speculated that perhaps she was angry with him, although he could think of no logical reason for it.

"No. That belongs to Adam, he's . . . he was a friend. He used to live here, but he's moving out."

Spock considered this information, along with what he'd already observed of her demeanor, and made the logical deduction. Intimate human relationships were generally based on mutual affection between two participants, the relationship ending if one or both parties involved no longer wished to pursue it. It seemed likely that Miss Kalomi had recently ended such a relationship.

Spock looked around the room again, saw several other instruments—brass-wind, wood-wind, something that looked like a violoncello. "And the other instruments? Do they belong to Adam as well?"

"He's studied music for a very long time," she said, her voice distant, her gaze fixed upon her computer's screen. "A few are borrowed from the university, but most are his."

"Music is a noble pursuit." Spock was uncertain of what else to say. He did not wish to make her uncomfortable. He decided not to inquire any further about the instruments.

Miss Kalomi nodded but made no response, apparently distracted by the task at hand. She typed in several commands, then leaned forward, undergoing the retinal scan necessary to access her university's informational database.

"The downloads will be completed shortly," she said. "Less than a minute, if there isn't a disruption in the channel. I get a lot of those."

"That is to be expected, considering the age of this building," Spock said.

"Really?"

"The relative positioning of field circuits has

changed in the past three decades, at least on
this continent. Previous relay systems required
a much shorter jump gap than what is necessary
for more modern equipment. The higher fre-
quency of the systems now in place will often
experience disruption during times of particularly high use, when they encounter the shorter
jump gap."

She watched him for a few seconds, then
spoke in a soft tone. "Mister Spock, is there anything you don't know?"

The question was almost certainly rhetori-
cal—Captain Pike had asked that very question
on more than one occasion and had made it
clear that no response was expected—but Miss
Kalomi seemed to be waiting for an answer, her
gaze lingering upon his own. Spock attempted
to comply.

"There are many boundaries to my knowledge," he said. "It happens that I recently read
an article on this particular subject."

She smiled, in a way that suggested pleasure
rather than scorn. "I just meant that you possess
an impressive recall."

He bowed his head. "I am"—he searched for
the right words—"pleased to inform you of anything you might find useful to know."

She was silent for a moment, her gaze still

steady upon his. He studied her eyes in turn, interested in the color. Statistically, such light eyes were a genetic anomaly on Vulcan. Finally, she returned her attention to the console.

"There *is* disruption," she said. "I'm afraid the download is starting over. I'm sorry, I hope I'm not keeping you from anything."

"It does not inconvenience me in any way to wait," he said.

Miss Kalomi sat on the end of a padded bench, nearly hidden by the array of items strewn across it. They did not speak for a moment. Spock looked about the room, noticed that there were, in fact, several instrument cases stamped with the initials of the university. There were six in all, and four other cases that appeared unmarked. The borrowed instruments bore proximity locks, of a more sophisticated design than that of the latch on the apartment door. The larger instruments were fitted with gravity devices. Spock was curious about the collection, about the owner and his particular avenue of interest, but refrained from asking any questions in view of his prior decision.

"Vulcans get married, don't they?" Miss Kalomi asked, rather abruptly.

The lack of segue made it a startling question, but it was one he'd answered before. "Vulcans of the opposite gender are betrothed to one another in pairs for reproductive purposes," he said.

Miss Kalomi nodded. "And that . . . works out?"

"Please clarify, Miss Kalomi. Do you mean to ask if this practice successfully bears offspring?"

"No, I just mean . . . well, is that how it was in your family? With your parents?"

Spock hesitated. "My parents were atypical," he said, and hesitated again. It was an extremely personal question and a subject he preferred not to speak about. However, there was no logical reason to avoid speaking of it, either. He was a Vulcan. His heritage was fact. It was fortuitous that the computer signaled its readiness before he felt compelled to answer further.

"The download appears to be complete," he said.

"So it is." Leila stood, retrieved the data slate from the downloading dock. "Here, Mister Spock. You may take this."

Spock received the device. "Thank you, Miss Kalomi. Shall I return it here, when I've finished?"

"You're certainly welcome to keep it, if you'd like to have the information for future reference."

"There is no need," he informed her. "My memory is eidetic."

Miss Kalomi seemed to catch her breath, very slightly. "Then yes, you can bring it back to me," she said. "I'm in most evenings."

She walked with him the few steps to the door, then held out her hand, smiling. When he didn't immediately grasp it—even after all his years around humans, the gesture had not become reflexive—she lowered her hand, smile faltering only slightly.

"I look forward to seeing you again, Mister Spock."

"I thank you for your assistance," he said, aware that his reply wasn't quite apt to her statement but unsure once again of what else to say. He found her company interesting and informative, as he found time spent with most beings, but quite suddenly believed that it would be improper to tell her so. Why, he could not rightly say, but decided that it would certainly bear further analysis at another time.

The nitrilin solution had been added to the small plot of soil by means of pinpoint electron transportation, linked through the lab's mainframe, the meter-deep container of prepared regolith enclosed in a tightly controlled force field. It was their first live experiment, and as the minutes ticked past, Carol found herself unable to sit still. She paced as the other members of the team talked quietly, as Dachmes transported the initial samples into their respective containers, as they all waited. The feeling in the lab was expectant, tense; even Troy Verne seemed somewhat interested. At least he had ceased bothering the team members with his unsought opinions about terraforming.

Carol watched as Mac carefully grasped a transparent aluminum test tube between his gloved thumb and forefinger, holding it up for Tam's tricorder reading. A half dozen additional test tubes, filled with varying levels of soil, appeared to be suspended in midair behind the two physicists. They were perched on a delicate stand that was wirelessly linked to the laboratory mainframe. The tricorder reading was a calibration test measure, and Tam and Mac both nodded at the data they were getting, suggesting that the equipment, at least, was working the way it was supposed to. Nearby screens blinked with pathways of rapidly changing numbers and characters, casting winking lights across the faces of those seated in front of them—J.C. and Leila Kalomi were also in attendance, as well as Carol's trio of grad students, the ones who would be coming to Mars with them. Alison Simhbib, the Martian geologist, hadn't been required for the first phase; she was the only team member not present.

Richard Dachmes briefly glanced away from his screen. "It will be another . . . twenty-two minutes before the final results."

Carol nodded, perfectly aware of how long it would take. She wished there was something she could be doing, *anything,* but the work—her work—had been completed. She could only wait. Dachmes shifted in his seat at his workstation, his nose centimeters away from a screen flickering with numbers, crunching and blinking as his fingers danced across the keypad.

Verne spoke up, stretching his arms behind his head, his tone impatient. "Why so long?"

Mac answered, much to Carol's relief. Troy Verne had worn out her patience about ten minutes after their initial meeting.

"We need to give it sufficient time to adjust to the atmospheric changes that will occur naturally after a chemical reaction like this one," Mac said. "Those changes will beget our second reaction, between the nitrilin compound and the newly formed atmospheric gases. There's always a chance that the process won't stabilize as we expect—"

"Right," Verne said, and yawned. "Well, be sure to let me know when something happens. I'm already late with today's report."

No one answered, all of them perfectly aware of the pull that Verne had with Kraden. Carol avoided looking at him as the time crawled by. She had no doubt that Kraden would be quick to yank funding if even the slightest thing went wrong at this point in the testing phase. She knew that she had the capacity to be perfectly professional about failure, it was just so unpleasant to actually have to do it.

Not relevant. We won't fail.

"It's slowing," Dachmes called.

"That was fast," Leila said.

"Too fast," Mac said, shaking his head.

"What's that mean?" Verne asked and was summarily ignored.

"Not necessarily," J.C. said. "One of the simulations showed a result that was nearly this quick. We chalked it up as an anomaly."

Dachmes's fingers continued to walk along the keypad with a steady, rhythmic tap. "And," he announced slowly, "there you have it."

"Stable?" Carol asked. She was amazed at how calm she sounded.

"We have stability," Dachmes confirmed. "The samples are totally viable, and—" His announcement was cut short by J.C. letting out a whoop.

"Success!" shouted Mac, and Carol felt herself being hugged amid a cacophony of cheers and squealing. Her team members clapped, laughed, jumped up and down. Even Tam was smiling broadly, hugging herself, and Leila, who had seemed so miserable only a few days earlier, was practically glowing.

The results were checked and double-checked, the results coming back the same. Inception would work. Inception *had* worked.

"We have to celebrate," J.C. said, grinning. "Come on, Doc! Let's get out of here! First bottle of wine's on me!"

Carol shook her head. "There's still so much to do—"

"—And we can do it tomorrow, can't we?" Leila said. She stepped closer to Carol, lowering her voice slightly. "What's the saying, about making music while the sun shines?"

Carol smiled. "I don't think that's quite it, Leila . . ."

"But the sentiment's right." Leila touched Carol's hand, gave it a squeeze. "You deserve a few moments for yourself."

Carol glanced around at the happy faces of her team, torn for a moment. As a student, she

had always disliked working with the profs who
didn't know when to ease up, to let their teams
take a breath. She had promised herself never to
become one of them.

*But we still have to go over the analysis and then
break down this experiment, get it packed, and we
haven't even started loading the backup transport
assemblies . . .*

Perhaps she should stay behind; the rest of
them could go out, *should,* in fact. She started to
suggest that they do just that and was hit with
a sudden sense of vertigo, a light-headed rush
that made her rethink her decision. She couldn't
remember when she'd eaten last, she'd just been
so excited all day—and Leila was right, she deserved a moment or two, to celebrate, to relax,
to enjoy the awareness that everything was on
track.

To eat.

"You talked me into it," she told Leila, who
smiled prettily. Carol was pleased by the change
in the girl, by the light in her eyes. The botanist had seemed so much happier over the past
few days, Carol was starting to rethink her initial assessment, that Leila was going through a
breakup. She certainly doubted that she would
look so cheerful within a month of saying good-
bye to Jim.

The thought was a sobering one, and she discarded it in a blink. Today, of all days, was not the time to be thinking about that. Maybe a glass of wine or two would be just the thing, after all.

"And I'm buying," Carol said, raising her voice so the rest of them could hear. A cheer went up, and even Troy Verne had the sense to look pleased. Carol imagined that his next report to Kraden was going to go a long way toward making him at least slightly more tolerable.

Leila fumbled with her key card, and had to push at the sliding door with all her might. She'd had too much to drink.

But it feels wonderful, she thought, tapping a light panel and dropping her card on the table, wobbling only slightly as she took off her jacket. She hung it on the empty peg by the door, where Adam had always kept his, a tattered old thing that had been his father's. She wondered where it was hanging now, dismissing the thought in the same instant, feeling both melancholy and somewhat brave at once. Freedom. She was free.

There were all kinds of things she could really throw herself into now, if she was so inclined. There was the annual rain forest trip with Professor Bonner's group coming up, a full month in the field, and Bonner had invited her twice already. And she could finally dig into researching that spora design for her thesis, put in some real hours. Adam had often resented the time she spent immersed in work, and she'd cut down accordingly.

She suddenly remembered that Michael Haines would be going on Bonner's trip this year. He was the xenobotanist she'd worked with the previous summer, on Professor Asylle's nitrification project. He had been quite disappointed to learn that she was involved.

Freedom means options.

She looked over at the chair she'd cleared off for Mister Spock, remembered how poised he'd been, sitting there, his long arms folded across his chest. What had he thought of all the chaos? The apartment was clean now, Adam's things finally gone, her own put away.

And it's already time to drag them out again, she thought, with a twinge of sadness, *to pack for Mars.* She was thrilled about the project, of course, but a part of her wished she could stay here, at least as long as Mister Spock was—

Stop it. He's a Vulcan. Vulcans don't feel the way humans do. They're not like . . . like . . . But what *were* they like? Leila wasn't entirely sure. She had heard things, of course—everyone knew that they relied on logic rather than emotion, that they lived much longer than humans, that their blood was a different color. But they were also a very reserved people, which meant that relatively little was known of their culture, their *private* culture. The vast majority of Earth's population—herself included—had never personally met a Vulcan, and theories and legends abounded about what they were really like.

"Computer, on," she said. "Search. Vulcan."

Saying it made her stomach tighten. The screen began to flicker its results. She sat at the console, not entirely sure what she was looking for. She was a little overwhelmed with the quantity of material; in the two centuries since first contact, it seemed much had been written and said about Vulcans. She watched the words and images run past until something caught her attention. "Stop. Back."

Here was an entry about Starfleet, some kind of medal ceremony posting. It mentioned that there was only one Vulcan currently serving in Starfleet.

Lieutenant Commander Spock.

"Spock," she said, and his name illuminated slightly on the screen. "Select."

A list of dates and postings, a brief paragraph about his being decorated by Starfleet Command for heroism in the line of duty. Next to the article was a small image of Mister Spock in his uniform, his chin high, one eyebrow slightly arched. Leila smiled, recognizing his nearly ever-present look of curiosity.

"Spock, expand," she said. Roster lists, from the Academy, from his ship . . . and a handful of references that included the name Sarek. Leila followed the thread, curious.

"Sarek, Vulcan ambassador to the United Federation of Planets."

Sarek was Spock's father, it seemed. She briefly wondered why Spock hadn't mentioned it. Adam could never stop talking about his great-grandfather's fame and accomplishments in the music world, his much-hailed performance at Carnegie Hall; he generally brought it up within minutes of meeting someone for the first time. Of course, Vulcans didn't feel pride, not exactly. But—*why* didn't they feel it? Because they truly couldn't? Or because they chose not to?

She backtracked her search, looking for general information about Vulcans. She found an entry written by a sociology student, skimmed through it.

"Modern Vulcan civilization is based around the philosophy of Surak, a great thinker of his time, who

founded a movement which is now referred to as the
Time of Awakening—"

Mister Spock had talked about that. "Time of
Awakening, expand," she said softly.

"Since the Time of Awakening, Vulcans rely on
logic to solve problems that trouble their society, rejecting
any concepts or solutions that are derived from emo-
tional responses. Currently, the outward expression of
emotion is taboo in Vulcan culture."

Leila frowned, frustrated. That didn't tell her
if the rejection of emotion was an evolutionary
trait or a deliberate suppression. She felt strongly
that it was deliberate. Anyone who spent more
than a few moments with Mister Spock would
come to the same conclusion. Vulcan, perhaps,
but she couldn't believe that he didn't have the
capacity to feel.

She continued to read and search the pages
and pathways, but she couldn't find anything
concrete to support her theory. As the sweet
drone of alcohol slowly wore off, she began to
feel tired. She sank back into her chair for a moment, telling herself that she needed to sleep,
that Carol needed her at her best over the coming days, but on a final whim, she asked the
computer to pull up an image of Sarek. She was
curious to see if the son looked anything like
the father.

There were a number of digital images listed, even a few holopics. One of the larger files was titled "Vulcan Ambassador and Wife," and Carol quickly tapped it up, glad that she'd decided to look a bit further. Mister Spock's parents, how delightful—

Leila's breath caught. Sarek was handsome in a distinguished way, his hair silvering, his expression stoic, but it was the image of ambassador's wife that made her heart pound, that made her suddenly wide awake.

"My parents were atypical . . ."

The woman holding Sarek's arm was attractive, hair curled behind rounded ears, her barely lined face as kind and smiling as her husband's was serious.

Spock's mother was human.

Six

Thaddeus Kent regarded the swelling crowd with a twinge of unease, the sheer number of Starfleet uniforms making him a little uncomfortable. He was no novice when it came to public speaking, but this would be a little different from a Redpeace rally, attended primarily by rational, like-minded individuals. Almost all of the people here today were Starfleet, taught to adhere to a philosophy that ran entirely counter to everything that Redpeace and its sister organizations stood for. It seemed likely that he was in for a rough time.

If I can enlighten even one person. His nerves be damned. The years his organization had struggled to be acknowledged by the Federation, to be invited to conventions just like this one, would begin to pay off if he could get his point across calmly and rationally, if he could show that his was the saner view. His job today would be to broaden as many minds as were willing to open.

And this is *the right way to do it,* he told himself

firmly. *Getting our message out in this venue is worth a million Tyn Seis. A billion.*

As the seats began to fill and the throng of people entering the room thinned out, the moderator tapped on a voice amplification device. Kent took a deep breath; this was it.

"Welcome to 'The Cost of Expansion,'" the moderator said, his voice filling the room. "This is an open forum debate, so we'll be taking questions from the audience throughout the next hour. Those of you who wish to participate may do so by touching the square button on the right armrest of your seat. If you are called upon, please stand and speak clearly so that your section's receiver will pick up. Let's begin by introducing the members of our prestigious panel. To my far left is Doctor Bernard Ellroy, a Federation astrobiologist." The man stood and bowed, amid a brief scattering of applause.

The moderator introduced the others in turn, including two of Kent's associates—a young lawyer from United Environments and a xenobiologist affiliated with several causes—and finally it was his turn. He stayed seated, smiled at the crowd, and raised a hand in informal salute.

As the questions began, Kent quickly recognized that his earlier assessment of the crowd had been correct; the skepticism directed at the proenvironment panelists was open, to say the least. The lawyer and the xenobiologist were both younger and less experienced than Kent, and quickly became comfortable deferring to him. Kent took it in stride, doing his best to field each question with a pleasant, knowledgeable air. He wrangled with the astrobiologist on a couple of small points, felt that he held his own without much trouble.

It's going well, he thought, scanning the audience as the moderator sought another questioner. As Jess always used to say, he was "making the connection," putting a personal face on the cause. Although the questions continued to be less than open-minded, and were often too specific to really showcase Redpeace's ideology, the majority of the crowd was polite, listening respectfully to his answers.

A pretty young woman near the back stood up, her uniform showing her to be a junior member of the Federation Science Council. "Mister Kent, my name is Sarah Roth. I'm not sure I'm getting a clear understanding of what motivates you to pursue these goals. Is it simply that because you believe nature to be aesthetically pleasing, and you want to preserve its beauty, or are your aims more ideological?"

Finally, a question he could work with. "I

do find nature, in its pristine state, to be lovely and worth preserving for its own sake," Kent said, "but I am much more concerned about the long-term impact of environmental manipulation than just the loss of some pretty flora. For example, using an agricultural spray solves any number of crop problems, but we don't know what today's use of, say, chlorobicrobes will mean for tomorrow's soil fertility, do we? Simulations are not reality."

Roth was polite to the point of chilliness. "I understand why you would be concerned about such things—as everyone should be—but you do realize that all potentially hazardous chemical substances must withstand meticulous scrutiny before they can be approved for use? Countless experts work to ensure absolute safety. With all due respect, sir, I feel that your organization's aims are retroactive. Don't you feel that your energy would be better spent helping to improve the situation of—"

"—the situation of all living things?" Kent interrupted. "This is exactly what my organization advocates, Miss Roth. For all of the Federation's safeguards, I still feel that it's important to have at least one group making it their business to watch the watchers, so to speak. Consider the current situation on Mars. Without organizations like Redpeace, there would already be a half dozen new deuterium plants set up in the southern highlands, and who knows how many iridium or rhodium mines? Martian citizens have elected time and again to restrict terraforming, to ensure that Mars will not become a second Earth, with her overpopulation problems, her pollution issues of the last several centuries. The government pledged less than thirty years ago that there was no need to strip the surface for metals, not with the Main Belt mining so successful. And yet here they are today, ready to repeal that promise for a few more credits."

He started to bring up the terraformation experiment, but without the data to back it up, he didn't want to risk it. He could see that the audience was really listening now, paying attention in a way that they hadn't previously, and knew that they were finally hooked. He hit them with the line he'd been rehearsing for the last several weeks, one he knew would resonate.

"Does anyone here remember what happened the last time a privately owned company felt it had the right to Martian resources?"

Roth looked taken aback, and what seemed to him a majority of the audience did as well. Kent waited politely for Roth's response, aware that he'd scored big. In many ways, the Martian

Declarations were the very backbone of Federation law.

"I recognize that your intentions are in the right place," Roth finally said, "but I hear a fundamental misunderstanding of the possibilities of technology, and an inclination to assume the worst. It's as though you're driven by fear."

Kent nodded. "Fear is not entirely wrong, Miss Roth, but I like to think of myself more as a *concerned* person, a person who understands that 'progress' does not have to mean blind irresponsibility. I *am* afraid of what will happen if the Federation continues to allow greed and imperialism to take precedence over the health of planetary ecosystems."

"Not fear of disaster," Roth said, regaining her composure. "I meant fear of progress, fear of things that you don't fully understand. People nearly always react badly when first introduced to something new and mysterious. When vaccinations were first developed, many people refused to be inoculated against deadly diseases, fearing that they were 'playing God.' Just think of all the lives that would have been lost if that kind of irrational hysteria had won out over common sense, over science."

Kent changed the subject slightly. "And think of all the deadly strains of bacteria that have developed because of the overuse of antibiotics."

Roth raised her eyebrows. "Certainly you can't be condemning the discovery of antibiotics."

"No, of course not," Kent said. "Merely their overuse. What I condemn is the need to always defer to the science of man. When our attempts to fix problems simply create a new set of problems—"

A man in another section suddenly rose to his feet. "Then we'll fix the new problems," he said. He was young but wore the braid of Starfleet commander. "It's easy to criticize in retrospect, to point out failed chains of action-reaction, but no scientist, no engineer or researcher could possibly predict every single thing that could ever go wrong. By your logic, we should all sit perfectly still, never attempt anything for fear of the consequences."

"Well, you and I both agree that there isn't any way to predict what kind of unpleasant side effects are going to rear up when you toy with nature," Kent said. "Commander . . ."

The young officer lifted his chin slightly. "Forgive me for speaking out of turn, sir. James T. Kirk."

"I welcome your comments, Commander," Kent said, trying to mean it. Kirk had interrupted his flow, but the debate was far from over. "That's why we're here, after all.

"So am I to understand that you believe we should stop trying to improve the lives of the beings we encounter?" Kirk said. "That we should just . . . give up?"

Kent forced a slight smile, friendly, open. "Of course not. Only to acknowledge that there are often better ways to get things done. Take the genetic modification of crops, for example, starting back in the late twentieth century—"

"The results of which have never been anything but positive," Kirk said.

Kent laughed, unable to keep the edge of scorn out. "You call the near extinction of the monarch butterfly a positive result?"

"A butterfly?" Kirk said. "All the countries— the *planets*—that were rescued from starvation by GM crops, and you think we should worry about a butterfly?"

A low murmur of disapproval rose from the crowd, mostly Kent's supporters, but he could see that they weren't the only ones.

"This is exactly the kind of thing I would expect to hear from a Starfleet officer," he said firmly, confident he was regaining the upper hand. "If only Starfleet Academy would stress to their cadets the importance of the little things.

The universe, as vast and intricate as it is, can be thrown into complete chaos if something as small and seemingly insignificant as a species of butterfly is destroyed—"

"What sort of evidence do you have to be making a claim like that?" Kirk asked. "The Federation is interested in helping intelligent beings better the quality of their lives. The preservation of all species is important, of course, but where does an insect stand against feeding a billion hungry children? Or a billion insects, for that matter, to a single child?"

Another murmur from the crowd, but the reaction was mixed; a few people actually began to applaud. Kent hurried to get them back.

"Commander, do you know what a keystone species is?" he asked, hoping he sounded more amicable than he felt. "Take the beaver, for example. Did you know that the beaver, before it nearly went extinct in the late part of the nineteenth century, created a natural irrigation system in the whole of North America that could never be rivaled by the dams and ditches created by humans? Did you know that billions of credits' worth of damage caused by floods could have been saved, human lives could have been spared—not to mention the health of hundreds of species of plants and animals—if only the beaver population had been allowed to rebound before the twenty-first century?"

"We've come a very long way since the twenty-first century, Mister Kent, as I'm sure you know," Kirk said, not skipping a beat. "And I'm sure you also know that there have been any number of so-called environmental crises in the past thousand years that have promised to spell the end of life on Earth as we know it. And yet time and again, technology has been able to solve the crisis, so quickly and efficiently that most people forget there was ever any trouble at all."

The applause was louder now. Kirk was an influential speaker, Kent thought, but it wasn't hard to influence a group who already believed in everything you were saying. He squeezed the bridge of his nose between his thumb and forefinger, felt his pulse pounding. It was time to shut him down, to point out the folly of his beliefs, the danger of reliance on technological optimism.

"That's all very well and good, Commander, but if we continue to act recklessly, believing that technology will come to our rescue when we make disastrous mistakes, then what will we do when technology *can't* solve the problem? What will we do when technology *causes* the problem?" Kent's voice was beginning to sound strained, and he hesitated briefly, drew a deep breath of air, pushed Jess's face from his mind. He began again, choosing his words carefully. "Just visualize, if you will, a precariously balanced sculpture. Or piece of machinery. A house of cards, if you like."

Kirk folded his arms, wearing an expression of infinite patience. The look was infuriating; it was all Kent could do not to start shouting.

"Now just imagine what happens if you snatch an object from the center of that pile," he said.

Kirk smiled with his mouth only, his gaze betraying his disdain. "It all comes tumbling down around us, the sky rains fire, and it's the end of the universe as we know it."

Many in the crowd laughed as Kirk went on. "I understand the metaphor, Mister Kent, I'm just not convinced that it applies in this case, or in any of the cases that your organization argues for. I believe that progress is the correct—the better—path to take. We should always try to learn from our mistakes, but looking backward isn't the way to evolve."

There was a spontaneous eruption of applause.

"I'm not suggesting that we *look backward,*"

Kent snapped, the cordiality leaking from his tone as he fought to be heard over the crowd. "I'm merely suggesting that we exercise a healthy and responsible restraint. It's important to get a complete picture of what the outcome is going to be before we just . . . just dump a shipful of chemicals into the atmosphere."

"That's the kind of language that's going to get you in trouble," Kirk said. "We are talking about scientists here, not trash collectors. Nobody is going to 'dump' anything anywhere."

More applause, louder this time, and Kent had had enough. He felt himself going cold, the fury an icy thing. "Those were scientists who upended that load of chemicals off the African coast!" he shouted over the sharp, swelling sound of handclaps. "How very *scientific* of them!"

There were hoots of approval from a few members of Kent's organization, but on the whole it was clear that the crowd sided with Kirk, the applause left over from his self-righteous diatribe still echoing across the room.

"Gentlemen," the moderator broke in, "we're running low on time. Next question, please."

An aging woman stood and started asking the astrobiologist about some useless Federation project. Enraged, Kent clutched at his knees, trying to maintain an outward calm. He'd lost it, lost the entire debate by his derisive and childish comment. No one would remember the points he'd made, only that he'd been sarcastic and churlish at the end.

If I can enlighten even one person, even one, just one, if I can enlighten one person . . .

The mantra wasn't working. He felt the sting of humiliation, the emotional impact of the young commander's complacent expression. He was exactly the kind of man Starfleet bred, convinced he was doing the right thing even as the universe went up in flames around him. Worse yet, able to convince others.

James Kirk, he thought, committing it to memory, his fists clenching and unclenching.

Carol sat alone before her computer, unsteadily clutching a stylus in one hand. A half-eaten pear, her dessert, rested on a plate nearby, where it had sat untouched for the better part of an hour. She had lost her appetite immediately upon receiving the message from Doctor Halley at the University Medical Clinic.

Oh, God, Carol thought, still staring at the screen, still lost. *Oh.*

The results of her med scan stared back at her. Everyone on the team had been required to get a clean bill of health before going offworld, one of Kraden's contract points. Carol had not expected anything to come up, she was usually very conscientious about regular visits to the clinic. Of all the things she might have expected to appear in her test results, this was probably the last.

Fetus, the results screen told her. *Approximately thirty-six days. Statistical probability of successful gestation: .988.*

She was just over five weeks pregnant. That weekend they'd camped in the mountains, it would have been. Which had been about two weeks after that appointment she'd missed, the one she'd blown off as unnecessary. The one that would have double-checked her fertility levels, to be sure that the new implant was working.

Like it always has before, she thought, wishing she could be angry with someone else for the failure that was so obviously her own. Why this time? Why, after five years of no problems at all, had this particular implant not taken?

Doesn't exactly matter now, does it?

No. No, it didn't matter.

Separate links could be explored to tell her the likelihood of various heritable traits, her expected due date, information about genetic markers. At the bottom of the screen was a link titled *gender.* She raised the stylus, then lowered it again, as she already had any number of times already. To know the sex of the baby . . . She wasn't sure if she was ready for it to be real yet.

But it *was* real. She and Jim had made a child together, the very thing she had occasionally daydreamed about but had always eventually forced herself to quash when she reminded herself how impossible it would be.

Impossible. She almost smiled. Obviously, it wasn't—but it was too, in spite of the fact. Impossible to believe.

Unless I highlight that link, she thought, *make it real.*

Gender.

She looked back to the top of the screen, read aloud: "Your physician recommends a daily prenatal supplement." She touched the link, placed her order. Real or not, she had to do what needed to be done, had to make some decisions right away. Doctor Halley could recommend a good OB. She should probably get a reference for one on Mars too, just to be safe.

There were other options. The fetus could be removed, given to a couple unable to conceive on their own or stored for future implantation; there were developmental risks, but it was a possibility. Or she could carry to term, and give it up—

No, I couldn't. She knew herself better than that. She'd always wanted children, always, had never questioned what she would do if she unexpectedly became pregnant. There was no question now, either. But that didn't make it easier.

A child. Jim's and mine. Her eyes filled with tears, but she wasn't sure exactly what emotion she was experiencing; she knew only that it was making her feel light-headed. There she sat, unmoving, stuck with a stylus in one hand, but everything was actually changing. The research that she'd been born to do, the discoveries she wanted to make, the settled, happy life she would one day have after she saved a few hundred worlds . . .

A child would change that. She knew it as certainly as she had ever known anything, that once this child came into her life, seeing to its happiness and well-being would become all-important. Would Jim feel the same way?

Of course he will. You know what kind of man he is. He'll always do what he knows is right, and he does love you. He'll love this child just as much.

Carol thought, then, of the "Starfleet widows" she had known throughout her life, their orphaned children always so proud of their missing parent. It was rough on them, she knew it. Most Starfleet marriages crumbled under the pressure of the separation, unless both husband and wife had been enlisted, unless they'd been willing to drag their children from posting to posting, taking them away from their friends, their homes.

It wasn't what she wanted for herself, for her child, but she shouldn't just dismiss it out of hand. Perhaps Jim would settle for a permanent post somewhere, where they could have a house, a life together.

Another almost smile. Jim wanted to explore, he wanted a ship of his own, he *needed* it. Starfleet wasn't just a job for him; leading was in his blood. And she didn't know if she could bear being cooped up on a ship for years at a time with just a few hundred others. Or with Jim, for that matter. She needed her independence, and so did he. Such claustrophobic familiarity would certainly spell the end of them. There had to be another way.

Her thoughts were interrupted by the buzzing of an incoming call. Moving as though in a dream, she clicked it on without checking to see who it was.

"Carol."

She recognized the voice before his image assembled itself on her view screen. Jim's eyes were gentle, should have been a delicious comfort, but she felt only panic.

"Hi," she said, quickly rearranged her expression. She smiled, her heart pounding.

"I'm not catching you in the middle of anything, am I?"

"No," she said. It was automatic, and a lie. "Just getting ready for the trip."

"You're not busy at all, then," he said, smiling. *"Think there's a chance of getting away? I'd like to see you again before you go."*

"Oh . . . you will." She meant to be reassuring but realized that she sounded uncertain, or as if she were trying to be coy. He wouldn't like that, he liked people to be straightforward. She tried to think of an amendment to her listless statement, but nothing came. *I can't tell him like this, not like this—*

"You seem . . . distracted." Jim's smile faded, concern replacing it.

"Long day triple-checking results, and there's still so much to do before Mars. I don't actually have time to get distracted." That, at least, was true.

Jim smiled, a playful expression. *"You're not hiding anyone in there, are you?"* He craned his neck, as if to peer over her shoulder into the apartment behind her.

"Of course not, Jim." She smiled, some of her composure returning. "The only dates I have are with my laboratory. I want to see you, too."

"Can you make time tomorrow?"

"I . . . don't know if tomorrow's going to be good. I'm sorry Jim, I'll . . . I'll just have to call you, okay?"

He did not answer right away, only studied her with a slightly puzzled gaze, as though trying to read her thoughts through the view screen.

"Jim?"

"Yes. All right. Call me soon."

"I will," she promised.

"You'd better!" He grinned boyishly now, his charm piercing her heart. He almost looked as though he wanted to add something, but then his image abruptly flickered and vanished as he ended the call.

It was late. Carol powered down the computer, threw away the remnants of the pear. She made her way to bed and lay down, plucked restlessly at the coverlet. She needed desperately to sleep but doubted that it was going to happen anytime soon.

I can't tell him, not with the experiment happening, with him about to leave again, she thought, she decided. *But how am I going to* not *tell him?* She couldn't imagine spending time with him and keeping such a huge secret. She would have to avoid him for a little while, until she could get herself organized, get prepared for the conversation that would follow the announcement. The thought of it made her heartsick, but she couldn't see any other way to keep it from him. She wasn't the type to keep secrets, and Jim wasn't the type she wanted to keep secrets from. She wanted to be able to share everything with him.

She got up and went to her computer. Almost without a thought she brought back the screen she had been looking at before Jim's call. She picked up the stylus and outlined a link, watching as the screen blinked back its result.

Gender: male.

"A boy," she whispered.

"Mister Spock!" Leila Kalomi said, opening the door and beckoning him inside. "Please come in!"

Spock gave a slight bow, offered her the data slate she had allowed him to borrow. He was a little puzzled by her tone, her manner, as if she had not been expecting him.

"It was discussed that I would return this here . . . ?" he said, a half question. She had clearly indicated that he could bring the device back to her apartment, but the protocol of social interactions with humans often required some degree of uncertainty, an allowance for error. It was the polite form. And perhaps, after all, she had forgotten.

"Oh, of course," she said, taking the slate. She gestured for him to sit, and he complied. Having been invited, it was appropriate for him to stay a short while, to engage in conversation.

The state of the apartment was drastically different now. The unruly piles of clothing and personal items were gone, a few neat stacks of traveling cases in their place.

"You are preparing for your trip," he observed, as she sat across from him on the couch.

"Yes. And you'll be returning to your ship soon, won't you?"

"Yes. In approximately fifty-two hours."

"Will you be leaving then, on another mission?"

"The improvements will not be completed for approximately another four weeks. We shall remain in orbit of Earth for the duration of the reconditioning."

They sat for a moment in silence. It seemed their expected interaction had reached its conclusion, or would if he could find nothing further to say. He cleared his throat.

"The particulars of your impending experiment have proved to be quite fascinating," he said. "You have my thanks for the use of the display device, and for accessing this information on my behalf."

"It was absolutely my pleasure," she said, and smiled.

Spock dipped his head in response. He had found that bowing seemed to constitute a kind of common ground between Terran and Vulcan custom, a signification of mutual respect.

"I was particularly interested in the section on compound chain reactions in a controlled environment," he said.

"Yes, that was interesting. Although I must admit, I don't understand all of it. My part in the experiment will primarily be analysis of the final effect, the components of the readied soil."

"Particularly the level of microbial activity, I believe."

The young woman nodded emphatically, smiled widely. "Yes, that's right. The four key biochemical changes necessary for healthy soil—and healthy plants—are brought about by decomposition; microbial activity plays an essential role in that process."

"Nitrification, sulfur oxidation, nitrogen fixation, and mycorrhizal association," Spock said.

She started to respond, then hesitated. "You know more about it than most botanists," she said finally, the obvious hyperbole indicating pleasure with his response. "Are you . . . do all Vulcans possess such a capacity for gathering knowledge?"

"The Vulcan mind does differ somewhat from that of a human," Spock stated. "However, the potential for acquiring knowledge does not necessarily denote a willingness to do so."

She did not speak for a moment, appearing to consider his statement.

"Mister Spock," she said, her face coloring slightly. "I . . . I must confess, I have learned something about you since our last encounter."

"About me?"

"Yes. I wasn't intending to pry, I only wanted to find out more about you, and . . . I did."

Spock said nothing, curious as to what data she meant to disclose.

"I found some things about your father on the net, that he is a Federation ambassador . . ."

"That is correct." Spock wondered if she perhaps had learned something about his father that he himself didn't know. It had been a very long time since the two had spoken.

"And I saw a picture of your mother, Mister Spock. I found out that she is . . . she is like me."

Spock experienced the slightest pinprick of regret before he carefully manipulated it back to where it belonged. Perhaps it had been a mistake to fraternize with anyone on Earth while on leave.

"My mother is of Terran heritage," he acknowledged. Obviously, she did not mean to say that his mother was a botanist, as she was not. He could not surmise what this young lady's motives could possibly be in trying to learn the details of his personal life, unless . . . If she was uncertain of his character, had concerns about having shared her project information with him, it was logical that she might seek out references of some sort. He felt compelled to affirm to her that he had no motive beyond curiosity, beyond a desire to further his own awareness of developments in terraformation.

"Miss Kalomi, if you are apprehensive about having revealed the data of your experiment, let me assure you that I have no intent to use the information for any ill means."

She smiled again, but her smile seemed different now—how, he could not precisely say. "Of course you won't," she said. "You aren't that kind of man."

Confused and unable to interpret her tone, he studied her eyes, her strange, luminous eyes the color of Earth's oceans and sky. He knew that Terran eyes could sometimes reveal the feelings they were experiencing, but he was not adept at the reading. Something in her expression unsettled him. A memory surfaced, a memory that served no useful purpose whatsoever—of himself as a child, surrounded by other Vulcan children.

"You are no Vulcan," one said.

"You are a half-breed, a human," said another.

"Leave us, human. It is not logical for us to consort with humans."

Spock willed the memory, the distress felt long ago, to recede. It had been brought to mind by the look on Leila Kalomi's face, so similar to one his mother had often worn in his childhood upon hearing of such encounters between her son and the other children.

What was that expression meant to convey? Pity? Sadness? Disappointment? For a moment he could not look away from the young woman, she reminded him so of his mother. He was startled when she leaned toward him, her hand slightly extended as if to place it on his face or shoulder. He stiffened, recoiling slightly at the suggestion of her touch, and she seemed to freeze for a half beat before her hand fell to her side.

She said nothing, made no further action. Spock could not untangle the meaning behind what had just taken place or why he should feel such intense discomfort from it. Her deliberate attempt to touch him had been a small thing, and yet he sensed that in that slight movement something intense had been conveyed, accidentally or otherwise.

He stood up, aware that a curt exit would be socially inept but unable to deny his strong impulse to leave.

"I regret that I must depart, Miss Kalomi," he said, backing slightly away from her.

She stood, hastily moved to the door to open it for him, no longer meeting his gaze. The discomfort, it seemed, was shared. Her muttered good-bye was almost inaudible, and as he turned to thank her once again for the use of the data slate, she allowed the door to close.

Spock did not move for a moment, deep in thought. He found all of it most puzzling—her search for data concerning his heritage, his own reaction to her expression and action. And more puzzling still, the sudden presence of shimmering moisture in her downcast gaze as he had backed out of her apartment. He knew at least what that meant, but what had transpired to make her suddenly experience such profound sorrow? And most perplexing of all, why should he feel such responsibility for it, not even knowing what had occurred?

Such questions served no worthwhile purpose. It was best, he decided, that he would be returning to the *Enterprise* soon. Humans were an illogical race, and Leila Kalomi a prime specimen thereof.

Seven

Kirk sat back in his chair, puzzled, after Carol blinked off the screen. This was the second time she'd put him off in as many days, hadn't even wanted to talk. He knew she was busy, but there had been something in her tone that he didn't think he'd ever heard before, both yesterday and today. A preoccupation.

It's the experiment, of course, he reassured himself, returning to the report collation he'd been working on before his impulsive decision to call her. After a few hopeless minutes, he pulled himself up from his computer station and changed into his workout clothes. If he was going to think about it, he might as well let off some steam at the same time.

He considered, as he walked down the corridor, that perhaps he was being presumptuous. He couldn't expect her always to be eager to shuffle her schedule just to see him. But even as occupied as she was, she'd always made time to talk for a while. It was as though something specific had changed, and recently.

Could she have met someone else? He gave the thought up before it had a chance to take hold. Besides his confidence in her character, he knew that she hardly had time for *one* romance, let alone two. His only competition was her work. In his heart, he believed he knew what the problem was, he just wasn't sure if he was ready to address it.

"Maybe I should just marry her," he murmured aloud.

"Talking to yourself now, Commander?"

He whirled around, startled. Doc Evans fell in step beside him.

"Some say that's evidence of an unbalanced mind," Doc added.

"Others might say it's a mark of genius," Kirk said.

Doc smiled. "I'd like to meet these others. I can't imagine that they have a background in medicine. You're heading for the rec room, I hope? I could use some fresh blood at the chess table. Haven't seen you around much lately."

He *had* been scarce on the ship's common areas, preferring to spend his free time in his quarters. Much as he hated to admit it, he'd been waiting for Carol's calls.

"Sorry, not today," Kirk said, smiling. "I'm working on my strategy."

Doc laughed, turning down an adjoining corridor. "You can't hide forever," he called as he disappeared down the hallway.

Good point. He had to face it, he thought, as he stepped into the empty lift. He'd told her he loved her, and now she wanted what most women wanted—a man she could rely on, a man who was going to be *there* for her. But could he be there in the way she wanted? Neither of them knew, and thus the cold shoulder.

Marriage . . . To Carol.

There were certainly worse fates. On top of all the obvious reasons to fall for her, there was that inexplicable *something* about Carol that other women just didn't have. He loved the cadence of their conversations, both romantically and intellectually, loved her touch and smell and shape. What might it be like to wake up to her face every day?

He could see his own blurred reflection in the doors, his eyes appearing as dark, worried hollows. Was it the face of a man thinking of marriage to the woman he loved? He looked anything but overjoyed, and all he felt was confusion.

At the gym, he taped his hands and made a beeline for his favorite punching bag, the one he'd found with just the right amount of give.

Maybe it would make more sense to just end it, he thought as he began battering the bag with rapid-fire punches. He felt a pang of unhappiness as he tried to imagine what he might say. It would be especially painful to break it off with her now, after confessing to her how strong his feelings were. Although with the way she'd been acting, it wouldn't be a surprise if she broke it off first.

He paused, letting the bag swing back perpendicular on its hook, his hands still clenched in front of him. End it or propose—not much of a selection. It seemed unfair that they couldn't just keep doing what they'd been doing, indefinitely. In a way, they had the perfect relationship. The anticipation of seeing each other after such long separations worked like a powerful serum on both of them, making their brief trysts sweeter and more intense than anything he'd ever known. If only it was possible to stretch something like that out into the long term . . .

He gave the bag a good whack with his left hook. There was no way. He wanted to sign on for a long-term mission once he had a command of his own. A week or two of separation was exciting; a year or two, and they'd be strangers.

He still held out hope that he'd only had the misfortune to catch her at a bad time . . . two bad times. But even if she was perfectly happy with him, with their relationship, he knew a change was coming, one way or another. There seemed to be no point in continuing if they weren't going to take it to the next level, whatever that was.

He gave the bag a few punches, halfhearted at first, and then settled back into the smooth staccato routine, the bag thumping and creaking steadily. Was there any way he could convince her to come along with him? To raise a family on a starship? He tried to imagine the two of them together, out in deep space somewhere, and it wouldn't come. He couldn't see it.

Carol would never join Starfleet, anyway. The alternative, if he were to leave service, or look for a stationary post somewhere . . .

No. He sped up, belting the bag relentlessly. His arms began to ache, but it only compelled him to move harder, with more precision.

He needed to be realistic, stop his wishful thinking. He had always had a weakness where beautiful women were concerned, but he couldn't let that stand in the way of what he truly wanted to do, couldn't let it derail his future.

And why not? a maddening voice in his head taunted. *Which would be harder to lose? You might think it will be easy to forget her and move on, but if you choose Starfleet, you might live to regret that decision more than any other. Think of all the women you've met since becoming involved with Carol. Why is it that not one of them has turned your head? Does that seem like you?*

No, he admitted to himself, it didn't seem much like him. But then, he'd made up his mind to stay true to Carol. Distractions were easy to avoid, once he'd fixed on a course of action. If there was one thing James Kirk was known for, it was his stubbornness.

Maybe he should simply follow her lead, wait to see what her next move would be. At least he shouldn't do anything until after Mars. If it had to end, at least they could have whatever lay before them on the Red Planet.

It was a romantic thought, but he took little comfort in the notion of Mars being their farewell. With a final flurry of blows, Kirk expended what was left of his energy, tried to let go of the troubling indecision that he knew was destined to haunt him until he found his resolve.

The bag squeaked on its hook as he walked away, mopping perspiration with a towel slung around his neck.

"Boy, that bag must have done something awful to deserve all that," remarked a young man sitting on a weight machine. Tom Christianson, new on security.

Kirk smiled in response. "Actually, I believe that it and I are destined to become great friends."

"Well, if that's how it is, I hope you don't count me among your friends, sir."

"Not friends," Kirk said. "On a starship, it's more like family."

The ensign grinned. "Just as long as you're nicer to your family than you are to that punching bag."

Kirk couldn't resist a little good-natured shadowboxing in Christianson's direction. The young man laughed, the bright sound following Kirk as he headed for the showers.

As he dressed, he realized that the brief conversation with Christianson had helped to dispel some of his doubts. He was destined for command, he could feel it in every conversation, every interaction with the people on the *Mizuki*—with *his* people. However things turned out with Carol, he'd chosen his path for a reason. For better or worse, he knew where he belonged.

Leila hurried to the garden entrance from the transporter station, certain that she was already too late. Of course she would be: she had to be at a team meeting in twenty minutes, and he was due back on his ship in just a few hours. The chances of running into him within such a narrow time frame seemed infinitesimal. Life never worked out that way, at least not for her.

The decision to try and see him again was a spontaneous one, borne of embarrassment and . . . of hope, although she tried to tell herself there wasn't any. After their last encounter she doubted very much that he would want to see her, but she couldn't let him leave without trying to smooth things over. She felt a cold knot in her stomach, remembering the look on his face when she had moved toward him.

Not alarm, exactly, but it had been close, and it had shut her down cold. She should have known better than to try and make physical contact with a Vulcan, but it had been instinctive. She just enjoyed talking with him so much, she had ignored the cultural barriers. And now she owed him an apology.

Yes, of course. And when his parents met, did they too suffer through such misunderstandings?

It was her hope, whispering, and as she scanned the embassy grounds, searched for him, she let it speak. It was the same whisper that had urged her to find him one more time, that had made her choose the flattering dress she now wore. He had confirmed that he was the product of a mixed marriage, that he had human blood in his veins. He must, then, experience some measure of human emotion from time to time, mustn't he? She had *seen* it in him, in his eyes, in the tightening of his fine mouth when she'd spoken of his mother.

She wondered if his father was somehow extraordinary among Vulcans to have married a human woman. Perhaps, then, even the Vulcan side of Spock was different. How lonely it must have been for him, for one who was able to feel, lost in a sea of beings who did not. She couldn't imagine it but felt sure that she understood.

Her breath caught as he walked into sight. He was strolling down the garden path, his arms locked behind his back as he studied a wooded display. The excitement, the fear and anticipation she felt just seeing him again, knowing that they would speak! She clasped her hands together, tight, watched as he moved closer.

He saw her, straightened slightly. His expression remained dispassionate, but Leila smiled, unable to help it . . . Until she remembered why she had come, remembered what needed to be said. As he approached, she walked toward him, forcing herself to halt at a respectable distance as the words came tumbling out.

"Please, Mister Spock, I've come to apologize," she said, relieved that she sounded so calm. "I believe that I made you uncomfortable the other day when you came to return the slate, and I have regretted it terribly. I would never dream of doing anything to offend you."

"You did nothing to offend me," Spock said, not unkindly. He raised an eyebrow. "In fact, Miss Kalomi, I briefly considered the possibility that it was I who offended you."

"Of *course* not, Mister Spock. You've never been anything but perfectly polite and kind and helpful . . ." She trailed off self-consciously as she heard herself, heard the relief, the girlish admiration, and then laughed, feeling almost giddy in his presence. "I'm sorry, Mister Spock, you must think me an absolute fool."

"On the contrary, Miss Kalomi. I admire you as a fellow scientist, and I hold your current pursuits in very high regard."

"It means so much to me to hear that from you," she said.

"You honor me, Miss Kalomi." Spock bowed his head.

Leila felt herself blush as she stepped closer to him. It had been silly of her to worry so; Spock was a reasonable, a *logical* man. "I'm so glad to see you," she said. "I was afraid you'd already returned to your ship."

"Was there something else you wished to discuss?" Spock asked.

She fumbled for an answer. "Well, yes . . . that is to say . . . I mean, I just hoped to . . . see you again before you left. To talk with you."

Spock waited, presumably for an actual response. Leila cleared her throat, tried again. "On Earth, most people, when we enjoy one another's company, we might . . . deliberately seek one another out, to, to . . ."

"To discuss topics of common interest?" he finished for her.

Leila relaxed. "Yes, that's right."

"It is not uncommon for Vulcans to do the same."

Leila nodded, felt her throat going dry. She was suddenly near certain that he had come here as she had, on the chance that they might meet again. She looked up at him, and he met her gaze, just as he had done in her apartment, staring searchingly into her face.

It seemed such an intimacy, the intensity of sincerity, of quiet brilliance in his dark eyes. Leila could not let the opportunity pass.

"Mister Spock," she said, her heart hammering, "I must know. If you are indeed half human, do you not experience emotion as humans do?"

"Vulcan genetic structure is generally dominant in the case of mixed-heritage individuals, and so I am predominantly Vulcan," he said, his voice free of feeling of any kind.

Leila regarded him doubtfully. Was this his pat response? Had he learned to deny his heritage? Had it caused him pain, as she believed? She looked into his dark eyes, and he looked back at her with deep scrutiny. She felt weak.

"Was it difficult for you, Mister Spock?" she finally asked.

"May I ask to what you are referring, Miss Kalomi?"

"Being different?"

Spock paused, apparently considering his answer before speaking. "There were adjustments that had to be made, but on the whole, my upbringing was unremarkable."

"But . . . don't you feel anything at all, Mister Spock? You are, after all, half human. Can't you . . ."

"I chose to be as a Vulcan when I was a child. I do not experience emotions as humans do."

"You *do* not, Mister Spock? Or you *will* not?"

"I am not certain that there is a distinction, Miss Kalomi."

"There *is* a distinction," she said stubbornly.

"Vulcans employ biocontrol techniques to subdue their emotions," he said. "The process, begun in infancy, does inhibit certain neural pathways. By adulthood, the *choice* and the capability become almost as one."

"But you are not just a Vulcan," Leila insisted, her voice softening. "You are half human. Hasn't that caused you turmoil, Mister Spock? Haven't you ever been . . . lonely?"

She put out her hand, and this time he did not freeze or step away as he had in her apartment. She placed her palm on his chest, searched for his heart, but was unable to find it. He stood still for a moment, and then shifted his weight almost imperceptibly backward. She pulled her hand away.

"It is common among humans, to . . . to engage in physical contact as a sign of affection," she said. "Or friendship," she amended quickly.

Spock replaced his hands behind his back. "I cannot experience affection," he told her, and she felt her heart ache a little. "But," he added, "it is agreeable to me that you would consider me to be your friend."

She smiled, shifted her gaze to the ground.
"It is . . . agreeable to me to hear you say so."

Still looking down, she caught sight of her
timepiece. She was late, she had to go.

"I'm sorry, Mister Spock." She worked to
keep her voice even. "I have to leave you now.
It has been a pleasure, a great pleasure, to have
made your acquaintance."

She extended her hand again before remembering the awkward moment in her apartment,
but this time he took her hand, grasped her fingers gently. His skin was very cool. She knew
that his home planet was much warmer than
Earth; was it cold for him here? Scarcely real-
izing what she was doing, she moved closer to
him, nearly embracing him, as she would have
done to a friend in farewell. He endured it
stiffly, and she quickly stepped back.

"Mister Spock, again, I hope I haven't . . .
when we say good-bye on Earth—"

"Please, Miss Kalomi. There is no need for
an apology. Our cultures are disparate; misunderstanding is inevitable. It is no fault of either
of us."

The two walked down the path in silence.
Leila fought away tears as the transporter came
into view. This could be the last time that she
would ever speak to Mister Spock in person. As

brief and confusing as their time together had been, she had grown quite attached to him.

If only I could tell him . . .

Tell him what, exactly? She didn't know, wasn't sure.

Spock bowed again as Leila stepped into the transporter, this time a more formal bow made from the waist. "Miss Kalomi, I am indebted to you for your generosity. I would hope that if you were ever in need of anything from me, you would not hesitate to contact me on the *Enterprise*."

He raised his hand, spread his fingers apart. "This is a traditional gesture on my planet," he told her. "A well-wishing."

Leila imitated the gesture, forming a V between her ring and middle fingers, extending her thumb.

"May you live long and prosper," he said.

"May you live long and prosper," she repeated, her voice breaking on the last syllable. The hum of the transporter enveloped her and she watched him disappear, his hand still extended in farewell.

Kent's head was throbbing. Another headache, ill timed as usual, but with what Preston Sadler was telling him, perfectly understandable.

He'd been back on Mars for less than a day.

"An injunction for something like this—it's just not worth the effort," the lawyer said. *"Even if I could get a judge to sign off on it, it wouldn't hold up under any kind of appeal."*

"So how much time *can* we buy?" Kent asked.

Sadler sighed. *"You're not listening to me, Thad. Even the proviro arbiters don't want to bother with this one."*

The lawyer hesitated, then added, *"I don't mean to sound apathetic, but this experiment is really pretty harmless in the grand scheme of things."*

Kent chose his words carefully. "The grand scheme of things is exactly why this experiment *is* harmful." He squinted at the too-bright screen, pulled back his aching head. He tapped the monitor's control panel, trying to tone down the yellow, but he only succeeded in turning Sadler's face a strange shade of magenta.

"I understand where you're coming from. Believe me, I do. But to get the courts to act, we'd have to be able to prove that Kraden means to irreversibly alter the landscape or atmosphere. All they're doing is testing some compound, in a small, contained plot of land."

"You just told me the compound was highly unstable."

"Yes, but it's Federation approved. We can't say boo about it."

"Can't we argue that this constitutes a first step in an irreversible process?"

Sadler shook his head, the motion sending shockwaves through Kent's line of vision. He blinked, tried to adjust the brightness once more.

"I'm sure the applications of their experiment will be contentious, but at this stage, we've got nothing."

"But they're changing the atomic structure of the soil—" Kent began.

"—and it's all under ground-level force field. Might as well try to stop someone from planting a dome garden."

"The unstable compound, then. Couldn't that pose a threat to the environment? Not to mention the *people*? The public at least cares about the safety of other people, don't they?"

"The Federation wouldn't have approved it if there was any real danger. I'm sorry, Thad, but I think this one is a waste of our time. We need to let it go."

Kent closed his eyes, tried to calm himself. "A waste of our time," he repeated, trying to sound neutral. His head was killing him. "Well. That's it, then."

Preston's face was still up, his expression a mask of uncertainty and a trace of sympathetic concern, but it was clear that the call was over. Kent snapped off the comm without saying

good-bye. The attorneys could give up, he decided. They could all give up. But there were
other ways to get things done, to raise awareness, to incite people to act. He would go to the
source, find a way to talk to the scientists themselves.

I won't stop fighting, Jess, he promised himself,
promised her through the pain in his head, his
fingers already at the keys, calling up names and
numbers. They might not listen to him, but
they'd listen to the people, they'd have to—and
he was just the man to make it happen.

Eight

The trip to Mars was uneventful. The team was excited and full of chatter, though Carol found it difficult to relax with them, spent her time ostensibly buried in a collection of data slates as star-filled darkness whipped past the chartered shuttle. Her thoughts were elsewhere.

She tried to shake off her guilt as they prepared to dock at Mars's main station, a Federation terminal. It connected directly to Starfleet's shipyard facility, from where they would be beaming down. She had known about the baby for four days now and had not spoken to Jim in person once. Carol felt like she was hiding from him. It didn't help that she'd figured out exactly nothing in that time. She kept thinking that she had to get herself ready, to be prepared. But for what? She still didn't know what she wanted to do.

I'll see him soon enough. Once the experiment is set, we'll have plenty of time to talk. The thought was bittersweet. She wanted to put an end to the agony of indecision and longed to see him—but she was all too aware that their days of carefree romance were over the very second she told him that she was carrying his child.

Until then, there was work to do, a lot of work; she needed to focus. She shifted her mind back into its proper gear and unfastened her safety harness, her hand grazing her belly as she did so, resting there for a beat.

The shuttle's captain appeared in the passenger hold before Carol and the others could exit. "May I have your attention, please?"

"What is it?" Carol asked. Her team members looked at each other, murmured their curiosity.

"I've received a communication from station security. There is a protest going on just outside the Starfleet facility . . . aimed at you, it seems. They're suggesting that you might want to consider staying aboard the shuttle until the situation is controlled."

There was a burst of anger, of indignant surprise from the other team members. Carol shushed them with one raised hand. She was also surprised but could guess what it was about; hadn't she been teasing Jim about it, just the other day? *Environmental issues*. It was ridiculous. Inception was an extremely limited soil study with no planetary implications, not at this stage.

"Aren't they on private property?" Mac asked.

The captain sighed. "A Martian court recently upheld that the pedestrian conduits are to be considered public domain."

Troy Verne broke in. "That's right. People are allowed to gather peacefully in the pedestrian tubes. It's happened before."

"But who are they? Why are they protesting us?" Leila asked.

"Since the government here voted to lease out land and approve resource tapping, there have been a lot of protests," Alison Simhbib answered. "There has been particular concern about anything to do with terraforming."

The captain nodded. "According to the communication, it's sponsored by an environmental concern called Redpeace. They were trying to bring an injunction against Kraden concerning your experiment, but it fell through."

It was the first Carol had heard of it, and from the exclamations of the others, she wasn't the only one.

Except Troy Verne seemed awfully unruffled. When she caught his gaze, he shrugged.

"Did you know about this?" Carol asked him. She knew that it wasn't professional to call him out in front of the team, but his look of resigned indifference was suddenly very much on her nerves.

"There's always somebody protesting something," Verne said. "Kraden is a popular target."

It wasn't an answer, but it told her enough: he had known and hadn't seen fit to pass the information along. Carol bit back her response, turning back to the captain.

"If they are allowed to be there, then security can't do much to make them leave," she said.

"They can if there's any concern about overcrowding," the captain said. "There was a situation last year during a tube protest that got ugly—three people were smothered."

There was a collective gasp.

"That happened only because they were cornered by security officers," said Verne.

The captain frowned. "The way that I understood it, the officers were preventing people from entering the tube for safety reasons. Those conduits were designed to withstand a certain amount of traffic; the engineers never anticipated mass gatherings. A few of the protesters who weren't allowed in became aggressive and blocked the way of several others. There was a panic, and things got out of hand very fast.

"Of course," he added, "Starfleet has increased security measures since then, so a repeat of that situation is very unlikely. If too many people show up, they'll be dispersed. To err on the side of caution, you may want to wait—"

Verne interrupted the captain again. "But Starfleet has no jurisdiction over people who are peacefully gathering in a common area, as long as nobody does anything to violate UFP codes. We could be here for hours."

Carol actually agreed with him. "The sooner we can get started, the better," she said. "I would prefer not to waste any time. I don't know about the rest of you, but I've seen enough of this shuttle. Any objections to running the gauntlet?"

There were none.

Silently, Carol and the others exited the hangar and made their way into an adjoining pedestrian conduit, the shuttle captain leading the way. The tubes were very broad, with enough room for twenty people to walk comfortably shoulder to shoulder, but it was easy to see how they could quickly become claustrophobic if too many people entered at once. The transparent ceilings had enough clearance for even the tallest of humans but were still lower than those of an average living space. The closeness of their reflections above them as they made their way down the corridor made Carol uneasy.

Shouts of *Keep Mars Red* echoed from the adjacent corridor with ghostly timbre, directly

ahead and to their right. Carol's pulse quick-
ened as the chants became louder, and the reflection of activity ahead of them was cast across
the curved ceiling of the tube joint. A handful of
people milled around on their side of the con-
nector, perhaps taking a break from the heart of
the commotion. Carol was relieved to see a trio
of Starfleet security guards stationed with them,
waiting, it seemed, for Carol's group.

Two of the guards stepped into the tube joint
ahead of them, the third falling in behind as they
walked into the adjoining area. The temperature
rose abruptly, the noise and activity a huge intrusion on her senses after the long, subdued
shuttle trip. Carol ducked her head and pinched
her shoulders in as they made their way through
the crowd.

They pushed past animated holosigns and
a cacophony of hoots and chants. Much to
Carol's relief, the mostly youthful group was
enthusiastic but not wild. Their well-meant but
misplaced views were shouted almost good-
naturedly at the team, more in affirmation of
their opinions than actual condemnation of
the scientists. Carol realized that most—if not
all—were probably entirely ignorant of the exact
nature of Inception. They were young and passionate and had likely only wanted an excuse for

a social gathering. Kraden posted the field experiment schedule on their net sites; someone had seen the term "soil alteration" and drawn all the wrong conclusions.

There was a row of uniformed Starfleet security officers guarding the entrance to the shipyard facility. Carol let herself relax further; a few more steps and her first activist conflict would be over. Several of her colleagues had endured similar run-ins.

She was within two meters of the doors when a tall man stepped into her path, blocking her way. He was well dressed and seemed far too old to be at such a protest, but he held a Redpeace sign in one hand.

"Are you Doctor Carol Marcus?" he inquired. Carol was taken aback. Of course, anyone who'd gone to Kraden's site would see her name and could find a bio and image of her easily enough. Still, it was disconcerting to be addressed by someone she had never seen before, especially in this setting.

"Please, let me through," she said, looking around for help. The trio of guards that had walked them in had moved away, were busy pushing the crowd back, and those on the steps probably couldn't hear her.

"Doctor Marcus, please. My name is Thaddeus Kent. Just a moment of your time. I have a few things to discuss with you that I believe you will find interesting, please. Just a moment."

"I'm sorry, Mister Kent, but I really don't have a moment." Carol attempted to shoulder past the man, but he sidestepped her and she could not move any farther.

The shuttle captain was suddenly at Carol's side. "Let us through, sir. Now."

"Doctor Marcus," Kent said, his voice polite and pleading. "I just want to discuss some of the greater implications of your work. Do you understand what your experiment will ultimately lead to? This is the very first step down a slippery slope that will irreversibly alter the landscape—"

"Mister Kent," Carol said, her tone flattening, "I really don't have time to discuss my work with someone who clearly has no understanding of what the *implications* are."

Kent was beginning to sound agitated. ". . . Because once you start tampering with ecosystems that you don't fully understand, there is no way to replace what has been lost. If you could just spare a *minute,* one minute—"

Only seconds had transpired, but it felt like an eternity in the closeness of the tube. More and more of the protesters were crowding in to listen, jostling and pushing to hear.

People were smothered.

"Let us go!" Carol shouted. "We are *scientists,* Mister Kent, if that means anything to you! We're not working for personal gain; we are trying to make things better for people!"

He tried to interrupt her, and Carol's voice rose an octave. "You talk about loss, you forget the gains! Don't you understand that sacrifice and risk are sometimes necessary to solve problems? Who are you to decide what's best for everyone else? What have you sacrificed that gives you the right?"

But Kent could no longer hear her. Security had stepped in. Several people were restrained, pulled away while the crowd reacted with a growing pandemonium, some fleeing, others trying to incite by pushing at the guards, shouting for action. Shaken, Carol accounted for her team and hurried them to the double doors that would lead to the safety of their work.

Spock's eyes would not stay closed. He opened them, regarded the sparse furnishings in his quarters from his seated position in the center of the room. He was having difficulty settling his mind into a meditative state. Disruptive thoughts excluded him from the calm he desired, an extended reflection of oneness. He decided that music might be helpful and stood, moved to retrieve his lute.

He adjusted the pitch of the instrument, stroked his fingers across the strings, but after a short time set it aside. The disruption continued, and it became clear that the most logical course would be to explore these thoughts in order to interpret their significance. Experience had shown him that this was often the only way to put such things to rest.

He was troubled by his last encounter with Miss Kalomi. He had begun to postulate a context for her actions and manner regarding their interaction. The curiosity about his background, her attempts to touch him, and the comparison she had drawn between herself and his mother—all of it suggested *shon-ha'lock,* the engulfment. It was a perilous emotional state experienced by humans, sometimes called a crush or love at first sight.

It was difficult to accept that the condition had him as its locus. He could not see how he had done anything, even inadvertently, to provoke it, but the evidence seemed conclusive. Humans were particularly susceptible when they were vulnerable, and the recent termination of Miss Kalomi's romantic relationship would account for the preexisting condition. In hindsight, he saw that Miss Kalomi had shown distinct signs of vulnerability.

Her attempt to identify with his mother encouraged an interesting issue. Spock had never considered it before, but now it occurred to him that perhaps his mother had experienced *shon-ha'lock* for his father. This would be a sufficient explanation of why she had chosen to marry outside her own kind. Spock had never been able to discern, however, any logical reason for his father's choice to wed a human. The implications had affected his life greatly, he believed, and there had been times he had resented it.

Spock felt a thread of emotion and allowed it to play out, identifying it as shame. It was not unfamiliar to him, but it had been many years since he had experienced it. As a youth, his resentment had shamed him, not only because he was ashamed that his humanity allowed him to feel emotion at all, but also because he knew that to resent his human side was to resent his mother, and his mother did not deserve to be the object of such rejection. As much as he had struggled for acceptance on his home planet, his mother's struggles had almost certainly been exponentially worse. In a carefully controlled sense, he admired her for enduring them.

He considered the possibility that his parents' marriage did have a basis in logic. Perhaps it had been his father's intention to stimulate social progress on Vulcan by introducing an example of an interplanetary union, to create a stronger bond between the two worlds by bringing the relationship to a societal level. Perhaps he had believed that eschewing tradition was necessary in order to change his own culture for the better—after all, harmony and acceptance were the loftiest of goals to a Vulcan, and a more widespread acceptance of Terran customs seemed to serve those goals.

And yet, the results of his parents' marriage would indicate that there was no logic in it at all. The children of such unions were not generally accepted into either human or Vulcan society, and altogether the marriage had caused more conflict than acceptance. It was irrational to create interference in the smooth inner workings of society in order to serve one's own personal ideals and notions of what constituted the greater good. The needs of the many must always take precedence over the needs of the few. *No,* Spock decided, *a marriage to a human was not a logical option.*

There was no sense considering such a thing for himself, even if he wished it. He was already betrothed to a Vulcan woman. Though he was not well acquainted with her, the day would come when he would be compelled to partner with her, as dictated by Vulcan tradition and physiology. He did not, of course, have much thought or opinion concerning his impending marriage, except that he would prefer to return to Starfleet once matters were settled.

After a moment, he rested his lute on his lap and began to play once more. His quarters were filled with the ethereal sound of the instrument as he plucked through the notes of two ancient Vulcan ballads. His mind was clear once more. A faint shadow of . . . of something remained, but he believed it would withdraw with the assistance of meditation. He rose, put the lute away, and prepared himself once more for a silent contemplation of oneness.

Kent jerked awake from a half dream that he was still on Earth, still at the summit. He stretched, blinked, stared dumbly around at his small Martian apartment, at the flat screen in front of him. He could not let himself fall asleep now, not when so much was at stake. But what was the use? Nobody would listen to him. He had been hunched over his computer station for the better part of the last six hours, trying to contact anyone who would agree to help with another protest effort, and his resolve was growing thin. After what had happened on the station, many of the established activist groups on Mars and Earth were withdrawing support, displeased by the negative coverage. The protest had been disorganized, a lot of young fringe elements banding together without a clear purpose, and the perception was that Starfleet had been forced to step in, to save lives. Kent had done his best to reassure his contacts, but to no avail. Everyone seemed to agree with Preston Sadler that the scope of this particular experiment was too limited to be of concern.

He deeply resented Carol Marcus's implication that he didn't understand the ecosystem. He'd read everything about the possible results of terraforming on Mars; he knew that the long-term environmental impacts were impossible to predict. A number of researchers had even warned that terraforming Mars would amount to a black hole for resources, becoming so consumptive that it would never be able to pay for itself, but Kraden refused to listen. The public was overwhelmingly in favor of science; they believed it could cure anything.

Doctor Marcus's refusal to speak to him, to spare him a single moment, was indicative of that mind-set, that blind allegiance to dogmatic boundaries—he disagreed with her and was therefore wrong.

What really burned—what had kept him at the computer, kept him focused throughout his exhaustion—was what she'd shouted as he'd been dragged away, hauled from the tube like some animal. What had he sacrificed? His wife, his beloved and best friend, that was all. How dare she presume to know his experience? What did she know about *anything,* buried in her tiny, inbred community of self-congratulating academia? It was beyond infuriating.

Redpeace had been officially barred from the space station pending a judicial overview, which could take weeks. That made further local public protest nearly impossible. He had been trying to convince some of his contacts on Earth to stage a protest at Kraden's headquarters, to pressure them into pulling funding, but he couldn't drum up enough interest to make a bubble. Terraforming was controversial, but even some of their most committed sister groups felt it wasn't worth the effort, the specifics of the experiment too "general" to invite real controversy.

He stood, intending to stretch, then abruptly sat back down again. He hadn't eaten anything in hours, too involved in his increasingly hopeless quest for help. Jess used to get so mad at him when he forgot to eat.

"I'm sorry Jess," he murmured. "I don't know what else to do."

No one cared. The apathy of these so-called citizens of the Federation was almost too much to bear, it was worse than evil or selfishness; at least those came with purpose.

He stood again and moved toward his bed, leaving the sound up just in case anyone returned his calls. Eating would wait; he was too tired to go through even the simplest motions of food preparation. He lay down on the bed, closed his eyes—and his computer signaled an incoming communication. The promise of support alerted him instantly. He scrambled to his computer station.

"This is Kent. What is it?"

The face that came up from a deep scramble was familiar, though he couldn't place it until he heard the voice, that youthfully arrogant voice.

"There's something we need to discuss," said Josh Swanson, the kid from Whole Earth. *"Can you talk?"*

Kent didn't respond, his tired thoughts racing. Swanson seemed to take his silence as assent.

"My contact on the Kraden project says their experiment is going to happen soon, and fast. If you want to stay out of the fight, you should end this call now. But if you're worried about what Kraden's doing . . ."

"I'm listening," Kent said.

Nine

Mister Spock set his glass on the end table, templed his fingers as he watched her speak. Leila was talking about the project, about their early successes. It had taken some coaxing on his part, but perhaps the wine had freed her to talk about her own interests, to set aside her self-consciousness.

Except it's his interest too, she thought, setting aside her wineglass. They had shared the bottle of wine, a light dinner—she too was a vegetarian—and now, as twilight gave way to evening, the last of the day's light filtering through one of the apartment's small windows, Leila could feel herself relaxing, letting her guard down. From the way Spock was looking at her, the way he pressed the tips of his index fingers to his lower lip, she knew that he too was allowing himself to breathe, to be at rest. To *feel*.

He moved nearer to her as she talked, shifted as though to get comfortable on the low couch until his leg touched hers. She could feel the warmth of his skin through her clothes and knew, with a sudden intuitive grasp, that the touch was no accident.

She faltered, met his gaze—and saw a need there that moved her in its intensity, its depth. It was a longing for understanding, for the freedom to expose his inner self. It was more than that, though, more specific—it was a hunger for *her,* and as she recognized it, felt it, her body reflexively responded. Her skin felt tight and warm, her breathing short.

"Miss Kalomi," he said, his voice soft and deep, his eyes capturing every aspect of her, learning her face, tracing her mouth, her throat, the lines of her body. He wanted her so badly, wanted so much to reach out to her, to touch her and—

"Leila, are you almost finished?"

She looked up from her position on the floor and saw Carol standing in front of her, a look of faint amusement on her face. A half unpacked case of leaded tubes sat in between them. They were alone in one of the Kraden laboratory's small storage walk-ins, this one directly adjacent to the main operation room. Leila could hear the voices of a few of the others in the next room, talking as they set up for the next stage of testing. The surprise protest from yesterday was still the topic of choice.

"Caught you daydreaming, didn't I?" Carol asked.

"I'm sorry." Leila blushed, but Carol raised one hand, still smiling.

"Don't be. I've been a bit distracted myself lately. Tell me, was it fame or fortune?"

"Ah . . . neither, actually," Leila said.

Carol arched her eyebrows. "Really? So, it must be . . . love?"

"I . . . I don't know. Maybe." Leila smiled. "I think so."

It was strangely exhilarating to say it aloud, to confess it to another. He'd said he did not feel affection, she knew it was presumptuous to consider such a thing, but the way he had looked at her at their last meeting . . .

I see him. I see his inner face, and he knows it. Whether he wished to admit it or not, there was a connection between them. She believed that he was thinking of her on his ship, now, perhaps puzzling over his own confused feelings. Since leaving for Mars, her daydreams had grown more complex with each retelling, more detailed—and in each retelling, her feelings for him grew stronger.

I am in love, she thought, reaffirming it, liking the sound very much.

Carol was still smiling, the expression almost wistful.

"There's nothing like new romance, is there?" Carol said. "It's all so extemporaneous. First date, the first kiss—that moment you realize you can't wait to see him again . . ."

She shook her head, as though shaking memories of her own. Her smile had faded. "Enjoy it while you can. Things have a way of getting complicated."

Thinking of Adam, Leila nodded. Although her expression was neutral, Carol suddenly seemed sad to her, as though weighed down by something. The experiment, surely. But considering the topic, it occurred to Leila that perhaps she too was having romantic difficulties.

"The feelings aren't so complex, though, are they?" Leila asked. "Loving? Wanting to be loved?"

Carol paused, then nodded, her expression thoughtful. "No, I suppose not. Love is love."

Before Leila could think of anything else to say, Carol was smiling again, backing out of the room. "We'll be ready to repeat the first-stage testing in about twenty minutes," she said. "If everything checks out, we'll be able to begin the initial field run by the end of the week."

"Even with the weather?" Leila asked. Troy Verne, Kraden's representative, had expressed concern over the conditions—though it wasn't

particularly close to Mars's perihelion, a dust
storm had blown up in the past week. The bulk
of it was well north of the lab, but Verne was
insisting that the particle count would interfere
with Inception's results. Ridiculous, considering the force field density they'd be using.

Carol sighed, lowered her voice slightly.
"That *is* with the weather. Technically, we could
do it tomorrow. But the casts say it'll all be over
in the next day or so. I suppose we can wait."

Things were moving so quickly. They'd
reached the lab only the night before, and already they were unpacked—mostly—and ready
to run the stability tests on actual Martian soil.
Ready, in fact, to run the full experiment. The
results analysis would take another ten days, at
least, but it seemed that Carol's initial estimate
of three to six weeks had been much too liberal.

"I'll only be another moment," Leila said.

"Take two," Carol said, and then she was gone.

Leila set back to work, determined not to let
herself get caught up in another fantasy. Once
she had the supplies unpacked, she should
go over her measurement kits again, make
sure they were set up to receive samples . . .
Except that she'd been making him the instiga-
tor, and that was wrong. Mister Spock would
never be so open, so forward . . .

He sat on the edge of the couch, posture stiff and unyielding, and she could sense his turmoil, the powerful internal struggle raging in his breast. His face betrayed nothing, but she knew. She knew.

"Miss Kalomi," he said, straightening his shoulders, clearing his throat. "I should go."

He would or could not meet her gaze, not until she took one of his hands, cradled it within her own.

She saw the confusion in the dark wells of his eyes, saw that he was alone, lost. She touched his cheek and he closed his eyes, almost as though the press of her fingers caused him pain.

"Leila," he whispered, her name a plea on his lips. "I don't . . . I don't want . . ."

"Yes," she said and went to him. He started to pull away as her mouth brushed his but then leaned in to their kiss, his powerful hands slipping into her hair, cradling her head as though afraid that she would stop and he would lose her.

Leila sighed, her heart aching with fullness. The daydreaming had never extended past their first kiss. She tried to imagine making love with him, imagine how he would touch her—with thoughtful intensity, with passionate precision, she was sure—but that part always blurred, always sent her back to the beginning, to replay that first moment of his release, his acceptance of his feelings. On one level she knew she was being ridiculous, indulging her silly, childish fantasies, but they also seemed so real, so possible . . . so unlike what she'd had with Adam. Her Mister Spock was *nothing* like Adam.

My Mister Spock, she thought, and sighed, wishing with all her heart that it was so.

Worn out and content, Jim moved closer to Carol, slipped his arms around her. The thin mattress creaked noisily beneath them, as it had for the last half an hour. He grinned, and she smiled back—but she seemed distant. It wasn't what he expected after her abrupt call, insisting that she see him right away—

—*or that spectacular greeting,* he thought. She'd practically tackled him as soon as the door was closed, and from her responses throughout their lovemaking, he believed it had been a mutually fulfilling experience. And now, though they were nude and touching beneath the coverlet, she seemed light-years away. He wanted to ask, but he didn't want to press her, fearing that one or both of them would finally be forced to acknowledge the futility of their relationship. Now wasn't the time for that particular conversation; at least, he didn't want it to be. He held her tighter, and the mattress creaked again.

"Not exactly four-star lodgings, I suppose," he said.

Carol's smile softened, relaxed. "It's fine, Jim. It's perfect." She nudged her head beneath his chin, her nose grazing his Adam's apple.

"Well, at least we've got a view." He glanced out the window. The storm was settling down on this side of the planet, allowing intermittent views of the star-pricked blackness to emerge through gusts of billowing red clouds. "Though you must hate it, considering."

When she'd called, she'd told him about Kraden's concern over the dust storm, that it had caused her to put off the experiment for another day or so. Jim wanted to be supportive, but he couldn't help hoping that the storm would pick up again. He wanted her to have as much free time as possible.

"Jim, really, it's very cozy. Anyway, you're lucky to have your own quarters, with the transporter so close. Compared to the lab units, this is luxury."

"I'm not complaining." He smiled down at her. "Not today, anyway."

She turned her face toward his chest, kissing him at the base of his throat before resting her head again. A shiver ran across his shoulders, and he held her tighter.

"I was worried about you, when I saw the footage of that protest," he said. "The organizer, Kent, the one who confronted you? I had a run-in with him at the Federation summit. Went head to head with him at one of the panels."

Carol pushed away, propped herself on one elbow to look at him. "That's quite a coincidence."

"Yes, I thought so. I pulled up his file when I realized it was the same Kent. He's been an activist for years on Earth, just moved to Mars recently. A passionate person, I gathered, very bright, very focused. It's too bad someone with his enthusiasm and drive couldn't have found an interest in something a little more worth-while. Starfleet, maybe."

"Maybe," she said. They both smiled, but Jim felt that distance once more, saw it in her eyes as she looked away.

He went on. "His ongoing tirade against science appears to be personal. His wife died of some technology-inspired disease twenty years ago, something I wasn't familiar with. You would probably know more about it, something that developed out of resistant bacillus. There's a treatment for it, now, but not when it first cropped up."

"Resistant?" Carol knit her brows. "From the overuse of sterilizing agents, maybe. That explains his agenda." She looked stricken.

Jim pushed a lock of hair from her forehead. "It *is* sad, but I think people ought to rise above their personal tragedies, have a look at the bigger picture. It's not healthy to remain so focused on your own problems that you forget everything else."

Carol let her head slip back onto his shoulder. "I said something to him." Her voice was low; she was not smiling now.

"I said a lot of things to him." He chuckled.

"No, I . . . I said something I shouldn't have. I lost my temper, I shouted at him that he'd never lost anything, never sacrificed anything." She shook her head. "I didn't know about his wife."

"How could you have?" Jim kissed her hair. "You can't blame yourself for getting upset when someone provokes you. He was obviously looking for a fight, and he got one."

"But he wasn't confrontational, he just wanted to talk to me. I wouldn't listen."

"Carol. Whatever Thaddeus Kent wanted to say to you was probably as relevant as that Kraden rep's worries about the dust storm. You're a scientist; you know you don't need to be told about your own research."

Carol sighed. "I could have handled it better."

Jim held her closer. "You handled it fine. You're under a lot of pressure right now, a lot of stress; you don't need anything else to worry about. Let it go. Let it go, and just . . . just be here with me, now."

She responded by clinging to him tightly. He tilted her face to his, to kiss her forehead, her cheeks, her lips, until he felt the sad resistance in her begin to ease, felt her respond in kind. He moved his thoughts aside and shifted his focus and concentration to their kiss, to the thrill of her bare skin against his. He wanted to make as much of this night as he could, wanted to remember it forever, aware that it might be the last they would ever have.

Carol transported back to the lab in the early hours, her feelings too complicated to sort through. She tried not to think at all as she headed to her quarters, the sound of her footsteps absorbed by the dark silence of the halls, but it was impossible to keep her mind still.

I had the chance, she thought, moving past the main lab, slightly disgusted with herself, with her cowardice, but it had been so *good* to be in his arms, to pretend for just a few moments that nothing had changed—

"Carol?"

Leila Kalomi stood in the lab's entrance, her slender form in silhouette.

Carol pulled her jacket closer, tucked her hair behind her ears. She'd fallen asleep curled up next to Jim and hadn't bothered to inspect herself before transporting back; she probably looked a fright. "Leila? What are you doing up so early?"

"Making tea," Leila said. "Would you like some?"

Carol started to decline. She needed sleep, more than the few hours she'd had in Jim's bed, but she found herself following Leila back into the lab, reluctant to return to her troubled self-analysis. She doubted she would be able to sleep more, anyway. The final experiment was too close, the storm all but past.

Leila actually brewed the tea herself, using hot water from the replicator and a blend of dried jasmine and some other flowers that she'd brought from Earth. She poured each of them a cup, explaining that making tea was a morning ritual for her, one she'd developed in her undergrad days. Carol accepted a cup of the delicately scented stuff and sat on one of the lab's padded chairs, Leila across from her.

Carol sipped the tea, smiled. "It's very good," she said. "I'm impressed. I usually can't even find the food slot cards at this hour."

"I'm a morning person, I suppose," Leila said. "I'm not usually up *this* early, but the time change has me a bit off my schedule."

Carol nodded. "I'm never up this early, if I can help it. More likely to be up this late."

"Like Adam," Leila said. "My . . . my ex-boyfriend was a night owl."

Carol smiled. "And your new beau? Is he an early riser?"

Leila's own smile was slow and secret. "I don't know yet. I would imagine so. He strikes me as the type."

Carol sipped more tea, wondered if Jim had a "type." He was so adaptable, adjusting his sleep patterns to whatever his shift demanded.

"May I ask, are you just going to bed?" Leila asked.

Carol hesitated, not sure what to say, but decided there was no reason to hide the truth. It had been Leila's inspired words about love's simplicity that had sent her running off to see Jim in the first place.

"Sort of," she said. "I've been to bed already, but not mine and not to sleep. I just got back."

"Oh, I see." Leila seemed both amused and flustered at once, a charming combination. "Well. I hope it was . . . satisfactory?"

Carol laughed. "Yes, it was. At least . . ."

At least what? The sensual, sexual aspect had been more than satisfactory, as it always had been with Jim, but was she glad she had gone to him, considering everything else? The things she hadn't said, the one thing that weighed so heavily upon her now? She thought of how safe she'd felt with him, thought of the love in his tone, in his eyes and manner as he'd touched and held her. It had made her believe that everything was going to turn out right, and if that was false, she had still believed it for a little while. That time had been a gift.

"It was," she said again, feeling a sudden kinship to the shy young botanist. "It was wonderful. Being with someone you really care for, knowing that he loves you—how could it be anything else?"

"I'm sure," Leila said. "It used to be that way for us—for Adam and me, I mean—but it's been a long time."

"Not much longer for you, though," Carol half asked, curious about Leila's situation. She didn't want to pry, but Leila obviously had a bad case for her "early riser."

Leila flushed prettily, glanced away. "Perhaps," she said. "I don't think he's very experienced in that area . . . Which is fine, I'm not, either—but it's hard for me to imagine how we'll get from where we are now to . . . to there."

Carol smiled. "It will happen in its own time."

"I woke up this morning thinking of him and couldn't get back to sleep." Leila ran a finger around the rim of her cup. "He's . . . he's very smart, and sensitive, and quite handsome. Strong. He's tall."

"Tall is good," Carol encouraged.

"We only met recently, but I feel I've known him for a long time," Leila said. "The way he listens to what I say, the way he looks at me . . . Perhaps he's that way with everyone, but I don't think so. He makes me feel special. Important. Adam wasn't like that, he—"

She broke off, shook her head. "He's nothing like Adam. There's something about him. I sense in him all sorts of things that he probably doesn't acknowledge himself. Loneliness. A need to be held and comforted . . . but also a need to protect, to nurture and care for another. Maybe I'm projecting a bit, but I know I'm right, too. I know if he'll only let me in, I can make him happy."

She laughed a little, shook her head. "Listen to me. I sound about fifteen, with my first crush. I know everything, and I'm not sure about anything."

Carol laughed with her but also felt a twinge of concern. The young woman was head over heels, and it didn't necessarily sound mutual. She considered giving some unsolicited advice, about exercising caution in affairs of the heart, but realized in the same instant how entirely useless that would be.

Consider the source, she thought, and laughed again.

"We're sailing the same ship," Carol said.

"But you said . . . didn't you say he loves you?" Leila asked.

"He does. But there are other considerations. We have different . . . well, he's Starfleet, for one thing. An officer."

Leila lit up. "Really? So is my friend. Sciences."

"Jim's in command. And he'll be a captain soon enough, and he wants to go DS long term, for exploration. I don't."

"Ah," Leila said. "That's too bad. I don't mind traveling. I'd go with my officer, if he'd have me. I don't think you have to enlist in Starfleet to travel on one of their ships. They have advisory contracts in the sciences. And there are always station postings . . ."

"But is that the life you want?" Carol asked. Leila seemed so certain, so sure of herself. "What about your career? A home?"

Leila sipped her tea, her expression thoughtful. "What I want is to be happy," she said finally. "And for me, that means making a connection. Having a real intimacy with someone. I think we could have that together, if he's willing. The rest would fall into place."

It sounded so natural, so unaffected and easy. Carol's own reasons for keeping the pregnancy a secret from Jim, for even considering their breakup suddenly seemed almost petty.

"You said he loves you," Leila said. "Do you love him?"

That was the question, wasn't it? Carol didn't rush to answer, considering the question for the millionth time. She loved Jim's smile, his charm. She loved his wholehearted commitment to everything he did. He had a sense of humor, could actually be quite funny at times, but the core of Jim was his heart: he was so sincere, so serious about wanting to do the right thing, always. He was a good man, a strong, responsible, caring man.

"I suppose I do," she said.

"You should tell him, then," Leila said.

"Tell him—" Carol almost said *about the baby* before she realized that Leila couldn't possibly know.

Leila nodded. "It might make him change his mind about things, if he knows the truth. Wouldn't it be awful if he went his own way without knowing? Without being able to make an informed decision? If he knows that you love him, he might . . ."

She trailed off, a faint smile playing across her lips. "I'm one to talk. I haven't yet worked up the courage to tell my officer how I feel. I'm afraid that he'll . . . that he won't be receptive."

"I find that hard to believe," Carol said.

"He's grown quite used to being alone, I think," Leila said. "I don't know if he can accept that there's an alternative. Not for him."

"Then that would be his great loss." Carol's tone was gentle. "And you're right about telling the truth. Keeping secrets is a little like lying to yourself, wishing for things to be a certain way rather than accepting how they actually are."

Even as she said it, she knew that the decision was made. She would tell Jim about the baby, and as soon as possible. It would change everything for him, but that was only fair, wasn't it?

Leila's smile was a bit sad, but resolved. "It's better to know, isn't it?"

"I think so. I *hope* so," Carol said.

They finished their tea, both thoughtful and silent as the dusky Martian sky lightened outside, final streamers of swirling dust settling to the ground. The storm was over. The day of Inception was at hand.

Ten

Leila elbowed past Troy Verne, not bothering to smile at him as she seated herself at the counter, picking up the partly assembled force field density monitor. She didn't want to be rude, but his constant presence was an annoyance, especially for Carol. Leila glanced over at the other woman, feeling almost protective of her after their earlier talk. Carol looked frazzled, her eyes shadowed with concern and lack of sleep. Leila wished she could say something reassuring, something that would allay Carol's fears about both the experiment and her uncertainty over her own Starfleet officer, but with the rest of the team present, Leila didn't want to bring up anything personal. It wouldn't be appropriate.

Of course, facts and figures were what she needed to be focused on for the next few hours, anyway. She and Alison Simhbib had set up their equipment for the second phase of the experiment, and now Leila was trying to lend a hand to the rest of the team without getting too much in the way. The last thing they needed in the unfamiliar laboratory was another Troy Verne. Kraden's lab was much larger than the one at Carol's university, but it was laid out differently, in a corridor fashion, making it difficult to pass someone without at least grazing your hip on someone else's thigh. Verne had taken to pacing up and down the rows of instruments and monitors, and Carol was becoming visibly agitated with him.

"So, when's the show going to be over?" Verne asked. He'd asked some version of the same question at least five times in the last hour.

Carol did not look up from the tricorder she was calibrating, with Eric's help. He was one of her tech grad students. "The 'show' hasn't begun, yet," she said.

"Right, I understand. I just don't want to waste any time getting my report out. Kraden's standing by, you know. This could be big for us."

Big for you, *you mean,* Leila thought. It wasn't a kind thought, but Verne brought it out in her. Ever since the success of their initial test back on Earth, the Kraden rep had been overly eager to involve himself, to act as if he were actually part of their team.

Mac, who had exhibited more patience with Verne than anyone else, motioned for him to sit down. "There's nothing to see yet. Why don't you have a seat while we finish setting up? Things will start happening before too long."

Verne lit on a creaky stool, fidgeting noisily. Leila returned her attention to her work, fitting together the components of the small, square gauge that would measure the force field's relative tolerance while the experiment progressed. This instrument relied on a slender magnetic sensor that needed to be set in place with a tiny clamp. The gauge would not tolerate transport with the sensor in place, and Dachmes had complained about having to reassemble it. He had asked Leila to do it for him, remarking on the steadiness of her hands, but she was having difficulty. A tiny green light would glow once the sensor was placed correctly, but it remained dim.

Almost got it—almost—there!

The light stayed off. Leila suddenly found that the rhythmic protest of Verne's stool, responding to his bouncing feet, had become impossible to ignore.

"Would you mind?" Leila asked, struggling to keep her tone pleasant. "Mister Verne? Could you . . . ?"

Verne looked at her, his feet still bouncing against the base of the stool.

"That's very distracting, Mister Verne," Carol said sharply. "We're trying to work."

Verne stopped, a petulant look on his face. A moment later, Leila finally got the sensor placed. She let out a sigh, smiling as the tiny green light flickered on.

"Good work," Dachmes said. It seemed he'd been watching her. He leaned across the counter and took the device, began linking it to the mainframe.

"Thank you, Leila," he added, looking back up at her, meeting her gaze directly for a beat. He dropped his own quickly, almost shyly.

Leila nodded and smiled, wondering if he might be trying to flirt with her. He'd mostly kept to himself in the short time since they'd joined Carol's team, but he had tried a few times to initiate conversation with her and had a particular way of looking at her that suggested . . . something. She wasn't sure, and didn't want to assume anything, but she wouldn't be surprised to learn he had some interest.

Too late, she thought, and her smile grew. Her heart belonged to another. It was a girlish thought, romantic and silly, and she didn't care a whit; it was true.

Still smiling, she surveyed the rest of the lab. Nearly everyone was finished with his or her task. The tricorders were calibrated, the sensors placed, the complex arrangement of compounds and amalgams prepped to be beamed directly to the waiting regolith outside. Inception would be under way in a matter of minutes. It would be a success, she was sure, would give her plenty to tell Mister Spock when next they spoke. Perhaps she should call him this evening, to deliver the good news. He had expressed so much interest, he would probably be pleased—if that was the right word—to learn about the results as soon as possible. Her heart skipped a beat as she thought of other things she wanted to say, things she might be ready to tell him.

Maybe, maybe not. What had seemed so clear during her conversation with Carol was now less than firm, her resolve having flagged somewhat as she considered the improbability of Mister Spock's returning her affections.

"Here we go," Carol said, expelling a deep breath. "Everyone keep your fingers crossed."

Everyone watched as Carol, Mac, and Eric began the transport sequence. There was nothing to actually see, but it would have been unthinkable not to watch, anyway.

"Start charting the numbers," Carol told Dachmes.

The lab was silent except for the tapping of

Dachmes's fingers on his keypad. Leila scanned the faces of her teammates, each one manifesting nervousness in a different way. Tam's mouth was tight as she fussed with her tricorder, her shoulders hunched. Alison kept touching her hair, hooking it behind her ears. J.C. rocked back and forth on the balls of his feet. Nearly all of them were transfixed on one or another of the monitors, knowing they wouldn't see results for a while, obviously not caring.

"Nothing's going to be happening for at least another forty minutes," Carol said. She smiled, but she too seemed anxious. "And I'm sure you've all heard that a watched pot never boils. Go get a cup of coffee or something."

Verne sniffed. "I've never been able to get used to food slot coffee," he said.

No one asked you, Leila thought, but smiled when he glanced in her direction, unable to help it. She tended to avoid conflict whenever possible. Adam had always said she was too nice to people, that she let them take advantage . . .

She realized suddenly that she hadn't even thought of Adam all morning, hadn't thought much about him in days, really, and the realization felt good. Affirming. She started to search for some parallel to Inception, something about new growth, life from lifelessness, maybe, and abruptly gave it up, too pleased with herself and the moment to try and designate it. It was enough simply to enjoy it.

Presumably inspired by the realization that Troy Verne wouldn't be joining them, the grad students and J.C. all headed out. Dachmes leaned across the counter, smiling at Leila.

"Would you man my station? You don't actually have to do anything at this point, just . . . keep my seat warm, I guess. Unless you want to come with me . . ."

"That's all right," she said, and walked around the counter, taking his seat. She smiled up at him. "Take a break. You deserve one."

"I'll bring you a coffee, if you like," he said.

"Oh, no, thank you. I'm nervous enough as it is."

He walked to the door, but before he exited he threw her a look that cinched it, that made her certain of his interest. She looked away, felt herself blush. It was flattering, of course— Richard Dachmes was intelligent, he had a nice smile and a quietly sardonic sense of humor. They shared many interests, as well, but there just wasn't any comparison to her enigmatic, brilliant Mister Spock. She didn't want to hurt his feelings, though. She'd have to make a point of mentioning a new love interest the next time Dachmes was in earshot. That way, there wouldn't be any awkwardness.

Verne heaved an exaggerated sigh. "So, what's going on? How will you know when it's all over and done with?"

There was a terse pause before Mac answered. "Well, right now, the atomic particles in the soil are responding to the colloid."

"You mean the nitrilin?"

"It's a homogenous mixture, composed of several compounds, but yes, nitrilin is one of them—the most important one, in this case."

"What's it going to do? Besides not blow us up, knock wood."

"An explosion is extremely unlikely," Mac said. "Even if it was a real possibility, the force field we're employing would be more than sufficient to dampen it. We'd barely feel a slight tremor."

Troy looked at him skeptically. "What about underground? Does the force field extend beneath your test plot?"

Leila exchanged a look with Carol, who shook her head ever so slightly. Obviously, Verne hadn't even bothered to read the simplified summary that one of the grad students had written for him.

"Underground, we've got a natural force

field," Alison interjected. "There's an impenetrable layer of permafrost about a meter beneath the surface that will prevent the process from continuing further."

Mac nodded. "Anyway, the sims indicate that our volume of solution will diffuse in capacity beyond a depth of one cubic meter, give or take a few centimeters, with the density change. If it went deeper, we'd have to deal with all kinds of geological issues."

"Like what?"

"Like alterations in substrata density, build-ups of expelled gas," Alison said, "or what the added density could mean to regional fault lines."

At Verne's look of concern, she added, "Which we don't need to worry about. Really."

The rep was silent for a moment, his expression thoughtful. "Well, so then, what's it going to *do*?" he asked.

Mac was becoming irritated, his indefatigable patience apparently coming to an end. "The intended results of this experiment are twofold. In the first part of the process, key elements will be released from the regolith, including oxygen, and the resulting reaction, the second part—"

Verne cut him off. "In layman's terms?"

Mac smiled sourly. He tapped a nearby monitor. "In layman's terms, all you need to worry about are these numbers here. When you see the number nineteen come up, the first phase is over, and you can report that we've been successful."

"Nineteen? Why nineteen?"

Leila chimed in, hoping to give Mac a respite. "The atomic structure of the soil changes quickly, as soon as it's combined with the elements in the suspension. The nadion levels in the nitrilin will experience a quick drop, and then a very gradual surge. It will slow down and settle on point nineteen. That's when we'll know that it's no longer volatile, that the nitrogen-oxygen reaction we want will be controlled. There are other factors after that—soil pore space levels resulting from the second phase, for instance, that's where Alison and I will come in—but those can't be measured until the initial reaction is stable. When we see point nineteen, we can be fairly certain of stability. And therefore, of success."

"Well, rah-rah point nineteen, then." Verne pushed himself from his stool, stretched, then wandered off to the far corner of the lab, where Tam was watching the sensor reads. Tam ignored whatever Verne said to her, her shoulders still hunched, her expression dismal.

Carol moved closer to Leila. "Should we save her, or offer her up as a sacrifice?" she asked, her voice low, her smile betraying her.

Leila smiled back. "I actually feel a little sorry for him," she said. "He's very far out of his element here."

Carol mock-shuddered. "Whatever his element is, it's not on the table."

Leila laughed. "To be fair, I don't like food slot coffee, either."

"No one does," Carol said. "Someday, they'll get it to taste good, but it's never going to be the same as real. Not like your tea."

Neither spoke for a moment, Leila pleased at the compliment, at its implications. It *had* been nice, to talk. Leila hadn't had many close friends in her life, had always been too focused on work, or love. But she thought that her propensity toward shyness might be changing. So much was, and there was no reason that the new Leila Kalomi need be lonely. Walling herself off in her relationship with Adam had been a mistake she was determined not to repeat.

Carol moved toward one of the lab's small rectangular windows, gazing out at the reddish sky. Leila watched her, felt a twinge of anxious excitement at the thought of Inception's next phase. She and Alison would be transported out into the test plot within an hour of verified stability, to collect the first samples and read the nanometers.

She turned back to the nadion screen, watched the numbers travel up slowly. Point four. Point five. Point four again. Point three. Back up to point five. It would go on like this for a while.

Her gaze dropped to her hands. She thought about the coolness of Mister Spock's fingers, when he'd taken the apple from her hand that day at the embassy. Perhaps when she called, she would ask him—casually, of course—about signing on to a starship as an enlisted. She wasn't sure if it was possible, but if it was, and if there was any way she could be assigned to his ship . . .

I wouldn't have to tell him how I . . . the depth of my feelings, not right away. But after we've worked together awhile, become close, I could—

"Hey!" Troy Verne's loud, nasal tone interrupted her thoughts. "Is it supposed to be doing that? I mean, you said point nineteen, right?"

Carol whirled around, and Leila stared at the monitor, the pathway of numbers, felt her stomach lurch. The nadion levels were at point twenty-two, and continuing to climb.

Carol saw the read and ran to the hallway, her

voice raised to a shout. "Dachmes! Get in here *now!*"

Even as she called for the statistician, the station's incoming line started to bleat for attention, accompanied by a taped computer loop, calmly insisting that the call was extremely urgent.

Leila felt frozen, not sure what was happening, aware only that something had gone wrong, very wrong, and that it seemed to be getting worse.

Once he caught the gist of the transmission that Karen Dupree had forwarded—which took about a minute and a half, thanks to Swanson's amateur theatrics—Kent rose from his computer desk, uneasy, reluctant to view the rest of the loop. He moved to the large, curved picture window in his apartment, looking at but not seeing the Martian landscape, and attempted to piece his thoughts together.

This doesn't mean anything. The kid is a fool, but he wouldn't sell you out. And no one knows what's actually happened, not yet.

He stared numbly out the window, looked skyward. Almost automatically, he found the bright "star" that was Starfleet's Utopia Planitia station, in orbit around the planet. There were

Martian citizens who liked to try and pick the satellite out of the sky, saying it was good luck to see it just as night was falling; some even taught their children the seemingly innocuous bit of propaganda as lore. As far as Kent was concerned, the twinkling satellite was a reminder of the ugly landmarks people had plastered all over the galaxy, marring natural perfection with their various ignoble pursuits.

He abruptly closed the drapes, sat down to think. It seemed that Josh Swanson had sent the press a long-winded taped statement, claiming responsibility for some form of sabotage on a "secret" Martian experiment. Although no legitimate press association had yet opted to air the statement, the free net had jumped on it, was aggressively broadcasting Swanson's declaration on every major link—without substantiation of any experiment at all, let alone one that was going awry.

Brilliant. The blind leading the deaf, dumb, and desperate.

He had known that Swanson was going to do something—something to delay, or even stop, the experiment. But sabotage had not really been on the menu, at least not as far as Kent had understood. Swanson had told him only to watch the links and to prepare a statement from

Redpeace, describing why terraforming Mars was unnecessary and possibly even dangerous. To be ready for an opportunity to spread the message.

He just said he'd buy us some time, Kent thought. That WE had access to the equipment, and he would make sure that it "didn't work so well." He'd certainly never said anything about claiming responsibility.

Kent went back to his computer, looked at the few lines he'd already written. *We condemn the irresponsible acts of a few careless individuals.* He tapped listlessly at the keys, feeling rudderless, unable to focus. After a moment, he called up the loop copy that Karen had sent, restarted it.

A dark room, a dark figure wearing a bandanna over the lower half of his face. Gritting his teeth, Kent watched.

"Action is the only language that the big corporations can be expected to understand," said the figure from the tape. *"That's why we have taken drastic measures in order to ensure that this experiment is a failure. Were my actions criminal or heroic? You, the viewing public, will be the judge of that. What is the significance of a few man-made laws in pursuit of the greater good? I have attempted to save the people of Mars the misery of a potentially catastrophic, atomic-level experiment. Besides the colonists, what about Mars's complicated*

and delicate ecosystem? What about potential life-forms that have not even been discovered yet? What about the archaeological sites that have never been thoroughly studied?"

Offscreen, someone hooted approval. Swanson—for there was no doubt as to who was behind the ridiculous disguise, not to Kent—seemed to take heart, his voice to grow in intensity and drama.

"Before you judge me, maybe you should be judging these so-called scientists, who are supposed to be helping people. Maybe you should take the corporations to task. They care only about the short-term effects of their actions. What are their motives? Getting all the resources for themselves. They don't care about people or any other life-forms. It's important for those of us who care, who don't want to live in a so-called progressive reality, to stand up and be counted."

Stung by his own words, almost the exact phrasing he'd used with Swanson back at that rally, Kent paused the transmission, stared at the angry young eyes over the mask. The statement was all redundancies past this point, disjointed and rambling rhetoric. Karen's accompanying message had related that while the Federation was not yet a hundred percent certain of Swanson's identity—the WE manifesto had been online for all of half an hour—they expected to have the tape's electronic signature unscrambled within hours. Perhaps they already had. It wasn't as though his outlaw "disguise" would stand up to Starfleet's recog technology for more than a few minutes. The kid was doomed. Kent dearly hoped that he would not be doomed right along with him, but he probably shouldn't place any bets.

Stop it. You're not responsible for what WE does. And it's not as though you really knew *anything,* he reminded himself. It was a gift horse, as the saying went, and he meant to abide by the maxim's admonition. He was finally getting what he wanted—media coverage on a grand scale, real time to tell the public the truth, to enlighten them to those things that had been obscured by the almighty Federation for far too long. He was going to have to take advantage of the opportunity in every way he could.

He went back to his press statement, reexamining, with forced optimism, Redpeace's course of action for handling the unexpected publicity. Of course, there was always the danger of being lumped in with the fanatics at a time like this, but if he played it right, the contrast between Whole Earth's crazed video bandit and Redpeace's smooth professionalism—as represented by his own calm, open demeanor, his well-prepared statement—could prove to be invaluable to the cause.

He forced aside his lingering uneasiness. Things were really happening now, finally. News of Kraden's botched experiment would hit the links anytime, justifying Swanson's tirade and lending credit to the obvious and overlooked truth—that you couldn't tamper with nature and not expect the unexpected. Mars could still be saved. It simply needed to be left alone.

With a little luck, he told himself, *that's exactly how this will work out.*

Carol issued orders as calmly and clearly as she could, her tone, her *mind* devoid of any feeling or interpretation. The time to feel what was happening was later, not now. Not while she had a chance in hell to fix it.

"J.C., do not take your eyes off those force field tolerance levels," she said. "Mac, Tam, get me the tricorder readouts on all sensor points. Everyone, I want an assessment in two minutes."

The sound of the incoming line was an insistent irritation. "Alison, shut off that damned comm, will you?" Carol snapped. She had to be able to *think*. She leaned over the mainframe monitor, started pulling up the reads.

"Doctor Marcus, do you want me to alert Starfleet?" It was Gabriel, one of her grad students.

"No, we have this under control," she said. "Dachmes, cross-check the numbers with the sims, the ones from the first test. And I need someone to prep the aleuthian." She looked around, saw that Leila wasn't occupied; good, fine, she could do it. As long as they had the neutralizing aleuthian gas, there was no *real* problem.

Two years of work, down the drain, she thought, discarding the miserable complaint as quickly as it had come. If they had to abort, they had to abort.

"We have plenty of aleuthian gas, but I don't think it's going to help us," Mac said, and Carol felt time slow down, could see the sudden blank stares of shock aimed at the physicist, the entire team turning their focus to him.

"What?" she asked. "Why?"

"It looks like the nitrilin levels have been tampered with," Mac said. "Someone measured incorrectly, or the transport may have malfunctioned—and because it's already begun its first-phase reaction, adding the gas could create unpredictable results. We know that aleuthian gas will neutralize the nitrilin on its own, we know that it will neutralize it as part of the solution—in the correct ratio, but—"

"This isn't the correct ratio," Carol finished for him. "How much was used?"

Mac's expression was grim. "Looks like all of it."

All. Carol ran through a few approximations in her head and cringed. The case they'd signed for from the Federation had held enough to run the test at least a hundred times.

"Can't we transport in enough of the rest of the solution to create the correct ratio?" Alison asked.

"We don't have the inventory for that," Carol said. "But we *can* add phelistium and aleuthian, a measure of vented CO_2 . . . ." The combination should render Inception harmless, beyond what it had already changed. There would be a slight alkaline differential in the outlying regolith, but nothing substantial.

Tam spoke up, her small voice carrying soft and clear. "We don't have enough."

"Of what?" Carol demanded. "What are we missing?"

J.C., his voice panicked, called out. "Something is not right with this gauge. I'm getting a very weird readout over here! A little help?"

Carol ran, banged one knee on the back of his chair in her hurry to get to him. "Talk to me."

"The manual gauge shows that the force field tolerance has dropped to sixty percent, but the readout says it's still at full capacity," J.C. said.

"The master read has the field at a hundred percent," Dachmes called, fear creeping into his voice. "But the manual gauge is the one to watch."

Carol read and reread the failing gauge levels before striding back to the mainframe monitor, trying to organize her thoughts, to address the most critical issue first. Containment was top priority. Somehow, the initial phase of the process had run past the designated parameters—was still processing. They had to neutralize it, and they apparently didn't have the means to do so, definitely major problems. But if the force field went down, the situation would go from *problem* to *crisis*. "Show me the readout."

"Here." Dachmes gestured at a small window on the boardscreen. "I should check the diagnostics, but I'll have to stop watching the nadion readouts, and I don't think that would be wise—if those levels get any higher—"

—then we risk a second-generation nitrilin-oxygen reaction, and if that happens, we lose control of the whole thing. The possibilities past that were dire, at best. The testing at this level had been specifically designed to infuse exactly ten surface acres

of pure Martian regolith with the Inception process, measured down to the permafrost. The process altered atomic structure, infused the regolith with the organic and inorganic components of a Class-M planet's soil, which made the processed particles heavier than the regolith in its natural state. An acre or even a hundred acres of "heavy" soil suddenly dumped on a planet's surface wasn't a serious problem—but what about a thousand, with a brand-new atmospheric tent to match?

Or a hundred thousand. Or more. A second-generation reaction could eat through the permafrost, spread in every direction. If the process made it to the oxygen-rich atmosphere of an established dome garden, it could conceivably pick up enough of what it needed to extend halfway around the globe.

"We need that field at full capacity," Carol said. Better to address the definite than the risk. Dachmes knew that already, they all knew it, but it was too important to be a redundancy.

Dachmes nodded once. His fingers flew across the keypad, tapping into the force field diagnostics. It popped onscreen, and Dachmes and Carol stood back in confusion. The readout showed no discrepancy between the gauge and the readout.

"Something must be wrong with the gauge," Carol said.

"Not possible," Dachmes said. "That thing is brand new, top of the line, and you know the manual is ten times more reliable than the readout. Anything could corrupt the readout. If that gauge says the force field is going down, then the force field is going down."

"We don't have time to run force field diagnostics," Carol said.

Dachmes's face was flushed. "So you're going to go with the readout because it's what you want to believe?"

Carol felt her control starting to slip, hung on to it like grim death. She brought the screen back to the nadion level readout. The numbers hadn't jumped, but they were still edging up. Numbly, she realized that Alison hadn't shut off the incoming call, that the bleating of the damned thing was still adding to the general din—or, rather, that there were now multiple incoming calls.

"We need to apply boosters to that force field," Dachmes said. "We have to bring in Starfleet. We need help."

"Doctor Marcus!" called someone from the hall. It was Leila Kalomi, sounding as if she might burst into tears at any moment. "There's someone here from Kraden."

Carol turned, bemused. "Kraden? How did they—?" She did not have to finish the thought; Verne must have called them. She felt her control slip another notch as a lanky man with an expensive haircut entered the laboratory behind Leila.

"Doctor Marcus, my name is Teague Williamson. I'm a public relations consultant for Kraden," he said smoothly. He sounded like someone used to being heard. "A press conference is being organized as we speak, and I'm going to need you to tell me what's going on here."

"With all due respect, Mister Williamson, I'm going to need *you* to get out of my laboratory."

"Doctor Marcus, media representatives are on their way and we don't have much time," he protested. "I'm going to deliver a statement, and I need as much information as I can possibly get. Now, what can you tell me about what's going on here?"

Here? They're coming here? Incredulous, Carol shook her head, silently cursing Troy Verne. "You'll have to spin it on your own," she snapped. "We've got a crisis on our hands. Gabe, Eric, someone get him out of here. Tam, what were you saying about the solution? What are we missing?"

Teague Williamson kept talking as Gabriel started pushing him back toward the entrance. "Doctor, you might be interested to know that an activist organization called Whole Earth is claiming responsibility for sabotaging your experiment."

Everything seemed to stop again, a brief, hesitant breath of time not moving, of complete stillness marred only by the ongoing alerts of the incoming coms. Carol focused on Williamson, somehow found her voice. "Sabotage? What—*how*?"

"We don't know," Williamson said. "Sabotage is the word they're using. Whole Earth didn't specify what they had interfered with. But as Kraden is the only lab—and yours is the only team—currently running any atomic-level testing on Mars, it didn't take much guesswork. Starfleet wants a statement, and so does half the free net, not to mention all the Federation News Service. And since something has obviously gone wrong here, it would be in your best interests to cooperate with your *employer*"—he stressed the word in a way that made Carol's teeth hurt—"and do what you can to play ball, so to speak."

Carol stared at him another beat, weighed her options before deciding to ignore him entirely.

Prioritywise, Teague Williamson could go fly a kite.

She turned to Tam again, saw that the girl's eyes were brimming with unshed tears. "What are we missing?" she asked.

Mac answered for her. "We don't have enough phelistium."

"Phelistium? How can that be? We needed equal amounts for all the planned runs."

"I don't know," Mac said. He didn't look at Tam. "I guess an oversight."

"If we get enough, can we successfully neutralize the . . . that mess in there?" Carol asked.

Mac pursed his lips. "I honestly don't know. Maybe."

They would have to try. It was their only chance at keeping the situation under some kind of control. Carol glanced at Tam again, fully aware that she had been in charge of substance inventory.

"I take full responsibility, Doctor Marcus," Tam said, her voice trembling. "I didn't think—"

Carol held up one hand, broke her off. Recriminations would have to wait, along with everything else that didn't directly relate to fixing what was happening out there.

My first project, Carol thought miserably, in spite of herself. *Damn it!*

"Doctor," Dachmes said, tapping his screen, and his expression, his tone of voice filled Carol with dread. She stepped forward, looked at the numbers, awareness dawning even as he explained.

"We've got our second generation," he said. "The process is breaching the permafrost."

Carol hesitated only a split second, hoping that they weren't already too late.

"Notify Starfleet," she said.

Eleven

Kirk paced his quarters at the shipyard, feeling helpless and frustrated and gnawed at by fear. The news had been all over the links for the better part of two hours, and he still knew as little as anyone else. He'd already been on the horn to Captain Olin, to Ben Yothers over at Starfleet Intelligence, even to the brother of a *Mizuki* tech's girlfriend who happened to work at Starfleet Command—anyone he knew who might know something, anyone he could get hold of—and no one seemed to know what was happening, if Carol's Inception experiment was even the specific target of the activist group. All anyone knew was that the group—Whole Earth, they were called—was claiming responsibility for stopping an experiment on Mars. He wanted desperately to transport to the lab, but Kraden had yet to make a statement, and since everyone at Utopia was officially on stand-by, protocol demanded that he wait.

Call, damn it, he thought, pausing long enough to glare at the computer screen. He'd left at least a dozen messages for Carol since the statement had first hit the net. If her experiment wasn't the saboteur's target, why hadn't she called back?

I should just go, he thought, not for the first time, his fists clenching. *Damn the protocol.* Except he didn't want to make things worse for Carol. If she was handling things, his presence would just be an unwelcome intrusion into an already-chaotic environment. As far as he'd been able to find out, Starfleet had not been called in. The last thing he wanted to do was make things worse.

His computer signaled a new report filed. He stepped hopefully to the monitor, but after skimming a few lines of dialogue and text he cursed softly, turned away. It was the same material rehashed, the looped statement, a handful of new details about WE's criminal history thrown in. Kirk found it all maddening. The links were sensationalizing the sabotage, even glorifying it. The offenders were getting all the exposure they could have hoped for.

They were running the statement again, the self-righteous tone of the young man's voice grating on Kirk's ears. *"We're tired of standing by silently while megacorporations decide what's best for the future of planetary ecosystems,"* the shadowy figure—Joshua Swanson, if Kirk's own contacts were correct—said. *"We've taken matters into our own hands, since the public's skewed perception of progress has blinded everyone to what is really important. These researchers are shortsighted in their motives. We knew that we had to stop them by any means possible."*

Kirk's mouth tightened, a flash of dark anger tensing him further. Nothing was being said about the experiment Swanson was claiming to have sabotaged. The report concluded by saying that a number of researchers and representatives from various companies working on Mars had already given statements, denying that their relative undertakings had been tampered with. Kraden still hadn't spoken.

He was about to extend his pacing to the hallway when the monitor chimed, an incoming call. Kirk scrambled for the desk, felt a wave of cool relief as Carol's face assembled on the screen, the backdrop of the lab curving behind her.

"Carol! What's happening? Are you all right?"

She shook her head slightly, as if to dismiss his concern for her personal well-being. Her eyes said it all, confirmed what he'd been afraid of—Whole Earth had done something to Inception. He straightened, lifted his chin; he didn't waste time repeating his questions, only waited.

"I need a favor."

As though she needed to ask. "Name it."

"Starfleet is on its way, and I need a go-between. Can you—"

"Try and stop me."

Carol's jaw twitched almost imperceptibly. *"Thank you,"* she said, and tapped at the line panel, disappearing without another word.

Kent waved a reassuring hand to the row of net-cams as he stepped up to the podium, aware that he looked conservative and media friendly in his new suit, a veritable Boy Scout next to Swanson's masked bandit. He smiled, felt the smile in his gaze. Writing his brief statement, the first in a planned series that would showcase the importance of the cause—of keeping Mars pure, as Earth once was, of showing the citizens of the universe how hazardous "advancement" really could be—had reminded him of that old adage about the end justifying the means.

This is right, he thought, he *felt,* waving again. There were dozens of reporters here, packed tightly into the newsroom of the largest independent net broadcaster on Mars. There were Martian and Terran correspondents, as well as representatives from news agencies outside Sol system. The coverage alone was worth any concerns he might have.

And I didn't know anything, he reaffirmed. Besides, when he thought about all of the future environments that might be saved, all the lifeforms that would be spared because of this single event . . . Sometimes one moment of clarity was all it took to create real change. This could be the keystone event that he'd worked all his life toward witnessing, toward creating. Conceivably, it could be a wake-up call for billions of blissfully ignorant minds.

Wouldn't that be something, Jess? His smile widened. If this turned out to be such a pivotal point in his life, in *all* life, he'd be sure that everyone knew who was really responsible, and why. Jess's death had always been a tragedy, but perhaps it would no longer be in vain.

A number of reporters called out questions as he waited for the room to calm, texted questions lining up on the airscreen in front of the podium. The news had broken only moments before, that Kraden had requested Starfleet intervention at their lab at Promethei Terra. There were no further details, although Kraden was apparently organizing a small press conference at the lab itself. Fortunately for Kent, that conference was limited to a handful of media reps. The rest of them were here, waiting to hear what Redpeace had to say. Redpeace, the one organization that had devoted itself entirely to saving Mars from just this very disaster. And the one organization that had been standing by with a prepared statement, ready to help lead the way.

Kent began to speak, his voice carrying well across the curved ceiling of the pressroom dome, settling the last of the anxious reporters. "Redpeace—formerly the Immutable Foundation, of Earth—wholly condemns the acts of the few reckless individuals who are responsible for this alleged sabotage. We do not condone the use of violence or destruction of private property as a means to convey a message, no matter how important—how critical—that message may be. While we believe that the preservation of Mars's natural resources is of paramount importance— as we believe that all worlds should keep access to those things which are uniquely theirs—we have also *always* believed that nonviolence is the only acceptable method of interchange."

He paused, nodded at a young woman standing near the door, a reporter for the *Aonia Press*. The small Martian copyletter was extremely proviro.

"Do you believe that Whole Earth's actions are justified?" she asked. As she'd agreed to do shortly before the conference.

Kent briefly mock-pondered the question before answering. "In principle, no. Destructive, illegal actions are never justified. But since we don't know exactly what's happened at this point—what action Whole Earth took, or why—I wouldn't feel right about trying to make a judgment. My own sources have indicated that Kraden was working with an extremely unstable compound, and that Whole Earth's sabotage was minor, committed only to stop this experiment from occurring. But until the truth comes out, who can say?"

As he'd expected, the clamor doubled, everyone wanting to know what his "sources" had given up. It was a calculated risk—Starfleet would surely want to know about Redpeace's contacts, as well—but the benefits far outweighed the hazards. He could always cite anonymous tips. And in the hours to come, the story of Kraden's experiment—their use of atom-altering substances in rented soil, which truly was an outrage and an insult to the Martian public—would unfold like a direct-dial soap opera. Redpeace would be remembered as a source of knowledge and reason amid the chaos.

"The truth will out," Kent said finally. "In any case, I want to make it perfectly clear that organizations that use violence to make their point are no better than the companies that fund these dangerous studies in the first place. It is our responsibility—not just as activists, but as people, as *beings* who care about life and the environment—it is our responsibility to educate and to inform, to teach. Not to disrupt. I don't feel that Whole Earth has a right to make that decision for all of us, just as I feel that Kraden has no right to change this planet—or any other—without the consent of all its inhabitants."

He put on a careful smile. "That will be all for now, thank you. Our netsite is open and operating, and I'll be available again for comment later this afternoon, at fifteen hundred hours."

"Mister Kent! Over here! What about Josh Swanson, do you know him? Is he the masked man?"

"Mister Kent, is it true that you personally attacked the lead researcher of Kraden's team?"

"Mister Kent, have you been in contact with any members of Whole Earth?"

Kent backed away, smiling, satisfied with his performance. Their netsite was ready for big numbers, and if he hadn't managed it already, his afternoon statement would hold enough carefully crafted insinuations to incite millions of drop-ins by the end of the day.

He had turned to step off the low platform

when the room fell almost silent, the sudden
lull almost as startling as a shout. A number of
the net reporters had touched their hands to
their ears, their faces going blank almost simultaneously. Incoming report, no doubt. Probably
a big one if so many of them were receiving it
at once. Kent hesitated, curious, as the first of
them began to report to the hovercam in front
of her, her voice the first in a growing swell of
sound and activity.

"I've just received a report from our correspondents at Kraden's press conference," she
said. "Stand by for footage."

Kent was besieged by a new round of questions. He ignored them, searched for the nearest
live netlink monitor. He located one mounted
in the far corner, surrounded by a growing pack
of onlookers. Kent tapped at the podium controls, channeled an audio feed to himself.

The screen displayed a tall young man in a
loose-fitting suit, talking in the quick, oily tone
of a salesman. A line running across the bottom of the monitor identified him as Teague
Williamson, a public relations exec for Kraden
Interplanetary Research. He stood in a small
and basically featureless room, presumably the
dome airlock for the lab where Doctor Marcus
and her team were working.

Where they were trying *to work,* Kent thought, unable to help a tingle of smug satisfaction. No matter what had happened, this had to be an embarrassment for Kraden, and for Carol Marcus personally.

". . . is under control—was never, in fact, beyond the control of the researchers here," Williamson was saying. *"Starfleet has simply been called in to assist in maintaining the highest standards in the investigation of this matter, as expected by every Federation citizen. Again, I'd like to emphasize that there is no danger. The situation is being managed."*

A shorter, younger man appeared behind Teague Williamson, his expression just short of absolute terror—drawing Kent's attention. Kent wasn't the only one who'd noticed. An unseen reporter identified himself, threw a question at the agitated young man.

"Excuse me, sir, can you tell me who you are and why you're here?"

His voice was high and uncertain. *"I'm Troy Verne, and I represent Kraden."*

Williamson actually stepped in front of him. *"Mister Verne was assigned to accompany the researchers to the lab, to ensure that all safety standards were being observed,"* he said. *"He is not authorized to speak on Kraden's behalf."*

The net reporter ignored Williamson. *"What*

can you tell us about what's happening at the lab, Mister Verne?"

Verne's anxious face appeared from behind the PR rep's shoulder. *"There's too much nitrilin, the force field can't—"*

Williamson's voice rose over Verne's. *"As I already said, Mister Verne is not authorized to speak for Kraden. The situation is under control. A full report will be released shortly. I thank you for coming."*

"Can you tell us what Mister Verne means when he says 'too much nitrilin'?"

"Mister Verne, what is nitrilin?"

"Is there an issue regarding the force field in use?"

Williamson backed away, crowding Troy Verne from the limelight, repeating his empty assurances. The screen went to text. Kent tapped numbly at the audio panel on the podium as the reporters in front of him began to shout with renewed interest, demanding answers he didn't have.

Kent kept his expression neutral, not sure how to react to what he had just seen. *Too much nitrilin* sounded threatening. It sounded dangerous, and dangerous was not supposed to be on the agenda.

"I'll deliver another statement at fifteen hundred hours," he repeated, backing away from the insistent questions just as Kraden's spin doctor had, doing what he could to quell his worry as he made his way out of the room.

After her call to Jim, Carol did what she could to keep her team focused, to keep panic and confusion from reigning. She assigned everyone a task, demanded updated reports every two minutes—and waited, well aware that there was very little they could actually do until help arrived. She only hoped that Jim would get here before Starfleet did; she was in grave need of an ally.

She had Mac contacting every university and private lab on Mars, anyone who might have access to phelistium. Alison and Leila were in an adjutant research room, reviewing any and all material on the nitrilin-oxygen reaction that they could find. Two of her grad students were watching the front hall, trying to keep both Williamson and Verne from venturing back into the lab, and she'd sent a tearful Tam to do another compound inventory. J.C. was still watching the force field density meter, and Dachmes was running diagnostics on the main reads; the discrepancy between the two remained. The Inception process had already continued twenty centimeters into the permafrost and showed no signs of slowing, let alone stopping. She supposed she should be thankful that the time frame from the simulated runs wasn't applicable to the altered colloid's effects; the cold was slowing things down.

Sabotage, her mind repeated, her arms folded tightly. Insanity. If this Whole Earth meant to "save" Mars from Inception, they'd done exactly the wrong thing. Although how they'd managed to alter the chemical compound—if that was what they'd done—was beyond her. The nitrilin, all of the preparations they had used had been under at least one team member's watch since before they'd left for Mars.

It has to be a computer affliction, she thought, *sensor bug, something in the reads.* No matter what Dachmes kept insisting about the mainframe diagnostics, there was simply no other option. But she kept watching those members of her team still in the main lab, watching them closely, aware that holding any one of them above suspicion might be a mistake. One among many, it seemed.

"Doc?"

She nodded at Mac, seated at the communications station. He looked like she felt—dazed and fearful. "Yes?"

"No line on the phelistium, locally," he said. "Nowhere near what we need, anyway."

She wasn't surprised. Phelistium's applications were generally agricultural, and Mars's dome gardens were largely hydroponic.

"Could we piecemeal it?" Carol asked.

"Maybe," he said. "It could take a little while, though—"

A call from the transporter room interrupted him. "We've just received Starfleet's transmission. The engineers are transporting in now."

Carol pressed her lips together. She knew Starfleet's reputation for stepping in, for taking over. Her authority, such that it was, was about to be taken away. It was almost certainly for the best. Starfleet had the resources to deal with the problems they were facing, but she and her team knew the material, knew the science. She couldn't help worrying that Starfleet wouldn't let her people do what needed to be done, that in their efforts to help, they might end up hindering, making things infinitely worse.

Now would be a good time, Jim.

In the *Enterprise*'s main designated recreational area, Spock sipped a cup of hot tea and watched three of his shipmates engaged in a Terran game that involved a stack of cards. After observing several runs of the game, he had calculated the odds against each player and now formulated that Number One would almost certainly emerge victorious in the "hand" being played. The nature of the game was such that a statistical anomaly could occur—adding the element of "luck" for the humans involved—but the probability was solidly in the first officer's favor, at least in this particular round.

"Beat that," said Yeoman Colt, scarcely able to contain her excitement. She fanned out her cards in front of her, displaying two pairs of matched numbers. The player to her right, a security lieutenant, dropped her own cards on the table with an expression of irritation.

"I believe I will," said Number One. She laid her five cards neatly on the table, the corner of each marked with the same small shape. A spade, Spock believed it was called.

Spock took note of the reactions of each player. Yeoman Colt smacked her hand on the table in a particularly vibrant show of human petulance. The security officer appeared amused by Colt's antics and began to gather up the cards and return them to their stack. Number One was an exceptionally even-tempered human, generally displaying a very low degree of excitability, but Spock saw that even she was compelled to display her satisfaction as she handled the multicolored plastic pieces on the table, pulling them toward herself with a restrained smile.

Spock drank from his cup, noting that human emotional characteristics had been of great fascination for him in the weeks since the *Enterprise* had returned to the Sol system. Only logical; Earth was considered by most to be the cradle of humanity. It had always been a topic of interest for him, of course, but more so since his involuntary exile to Earth's surface. Which led him to wonder if there was a definitive measurement for the increase in his absorption. It seemed too ethereal to categorize, at least in a life-form that did not cognate in linear patterns. He decided that it would be something worth researching, perhaps when he'd finished his tea. Since he wouldn't be returning to active duty for another twelve hours, he had ample time to engage in leisure activities.

Doctor Boyce walked into the room, smiling and nodding when he saw Spock. He nodded back at the doctor. Boyce made his way to where Spock was sitting, greeting the cardplayers as he took a seat across from Spock's.

"Doctor." Yeoman Colt nodded and rose to leave the room. Spock theorized that she preferred to be alone while her sensibilities continued to be volatile. He might have expected some other reason for her distress, had he not seen similar reactions to the game in the past.

Interesting that so much emotional disturbance could be caused by a game of poker.

"Well, Mister Spock," Doctor Boyce said, motioning at the teacup Spock held. "What is it this time? Some sort of miracle brew, no doubt? Everything that baffles the modern Terran physician can be easily put to rest by the introduction of these phenomenal herbs, is that right?"

Spock was aware that the doctor was making an attempt at humor. Presumably, he was referring to Spock's recent interest in different blends of Earth's tea, brought about by his meeting with Leila Kalomi on Earth. Miss Kalomi had mentioned that the concoctions of herbs and spices were often used in a medicinal capacity. In the brief time since his return to the *Enterprise,* Spock had researched and sampled a number of the established mixtures. He found the taste of most to be quite pleasant, although much of the research regarding the definitive effects appeared to be anecdotal.

"I believe it is called chamomile," Spock informed the doctor. "It has the proposed effect of serenity upon the imbiber. However, I have not been able to detect any such reaction."

Doctor Boyce smiled widely. "I sincerely doubt that any herbal concoction could make you any more serene than you already are. Unless it kills you."

Spock hesitated, considering the statement. From what he already knew of the doctor's character, it was probable that Boyce was still amusing himself, playfully jibing at Spock's established demeanor. Therefore, he found no immediate purpose in pointing out that there were, in fact, any number of herbal concoctions that caused measurable sedation, on Earth and elsewhere.

Spock took another sip, decided it best to ignore the comment. "Perhaps it is my genetic makeup that renders me immune to its effects."

The doctor nodded. "A logical conclusion."

Yeoman Colt reentered the room, her voice tinged with excitement as she spoke. "Has anyone heard about what's happening on Mars?"

Number One raised her eyebrows expectantly. "I haven't."

Colt strode to the monitor that was mounted to the far wall and switched it on. She browsed across a few links until she found the one she wanted, its report in midprogress. Two men standing in an airlock, surrounded by media members. One of them was speaking rapidly, his expression distressed.

"*. . . too much nitrilin. The force field can't—*"

Another man spoke over the one already speaking. *"As I already said, Mister Verne is not authorized to speak for Kraden. The situation is under control. A full report will be released shortly. I thank you for coming."*

Nitrilin. "Yeoman Colt, would you cue this from the beginning, please?" Spock asked.

"Yes, sir." The yeoman quickly tapped a command into the monitor's control panel, starting the report over again.

Spock watched carefully, collating the facts and doing his best to read the inferences. An act of deliberate sabotage had transpired, at the very laboratory where Miss Kalomi was working. The Inception experiment had not been a success. The correspondent who spoke for the company that funded the experiment, Kraden, was attempting to reassure the public that there was no danger present, but there was much, it appeared, that had been left unsaid.

Too much nitrilin. Spock rose from his seat, picked up his cup to return to the recycler.

"Where are you off to, Mister Spock?" Boyce asked.

"To my quarters, Doctor. I must review all of the materials relating to this incident."

"Really? Is Mars of particular interest to you?"

"Everything is of particular interest to me, Doctor," Spock said, nodding at the physician and the cardplayers before turning away, already formulating initial probabilities. Depending on the actual ratio of nitrilin to the other compounds involved in the Inception process, Miss Kalomi and her team could be in very deep trouble indeed. Not to mention the rest of Mars.

Twelve

Upon arrival at the Kraden lab, the Starfleet officer sent to oversee the operation—one Lieutenant Almanza, a solemn-faced engineer who looked remarkably like Carol's own father—had wasted no time in sequestering most of her team in one of the larger common rooms while his accompanying trio of engineers worked on the force field. He'd also brought in a security detail, presumably to keep an eye on the scientists, and a lone science officer—a research chemist, barely out of the Academy, by the look of him—to go over their research data. Only Dachmes and Mac had been "allowed" to remain in the lab, along with Carol herself. Almanza was polite enough, but already in the few endless moments since he'd arrived, he'd tried twice to coax her into a "one-on-one" discussion about Whole Earth's interference, away from the main lab floor. Carol was not about to let Starfleet dismiss her from her own project. She stalled for time, watched the reads over Dachmes's shoulder, hoping that Jim would show up before she too was carted off for questioning.

And it looks like my time just ran out, she thought, stepping back from the mainframe monitor as Almanza moved to join her. His expression made it clear that he wouldn't be brushed off a third time.

"Doctor Marcus, if you don't mind, we need to ask you to join the rest of your researchers in the common room," Almanza said. "Your men here can coordinate with our engineers for now, and—"

"I *do* mind, Lieutenant Almanza." Despite their scientific aims, Carol could not forget that the Federation's "enforcement" branch was structured as a military hierarchy, and they behaved accordingly. It was something she'd long heard about but had never personally experienced. "And I'm surprised you're still asking me. You need me here, where I can actually be of some help."

The lieutenant's smile was placatory. "Doctor, it's extremely important for us to ensure that no one on your team was responsible for tampering with your solution or your equipment."

"My researchers had nothing to do with this," she said, hoping it was true. It *felt* true. "And neither did I. In any case, now is not the time to worry about *how* this happened. We need to repair it, and I need my team to do it."

"Whoever interfered with your experiment

may well have done so from this very laboratory. We have to conduct questioning, if not now—"

"—then later," Carol finished. "I am not going to abandon my work. If we can locate enough phelistium, I believe we can neutralize the process."

"We've got our people working on the force field system, Doctor. I assure you, we will notify you when we've managed to contain the solution. You can worry about the phelistium then."

What was the adage, about how if you had a hammer, everything looked like a nail? Carol shook her head, frustrated. "You're an engineer, Lieutenant, and you want to concentrate on what you know; that's fine. What *I* know is that the problem here has more than one facet. I appreciate the help you're giving us, but perhaps you should leave the science to the scientists."

For the indignation in her response, she *was* grateful. The engineers had already managed to determine that the force field was running at full capacity. Apparently the saboteurs had corrupted the readouts on the tolerance gauge, hoping to throw a proverbial monkey wrench into the experiment, but the force field itself had been running at full capacity all along. Unfortunately, the high-density field had been designed to contain the mixture only to a depth of four meters—three more than they thought they'd need—and it did not have the capacity to surround the solution on all sides. It couldn't; even if they had the exact specifications of strata density, the Pauli Exclusion Principle wouldn't allow both the force field and the parent rock material to occupy the same space. The permafrost should have stopped it underneath, would have if not for Whole Earth's interference with the nitrilin ratio—which she still didn't understand. How had they gotten to it? Almanza's team could extend the depth of the force field but couldn't do anything about stopping Inception's downward progress. They just seemed to be hopeful that it would burn itself out, which, to Carol's eyes, wasn't looking likely at all. The nadion levels were at point twenty-six. The second-gen reaction, caused by the unexpected atmospheric gases, meant plenty of energy. The process was continuing to press through the permafrost, and by Alison's calculations it could and likely would trigger a seismic event if it was not stopped within the next fifty-two hours.

Not that we have fifty-two hours. Nowhere near. The Federation would have to declare a disaster long before that. All of the nearby colonies would have to be evacuated.

"The rest of your team has been willing to cooperate," Almanza said. "I'm going to ask you one more time."

"Then you'll have to hear my refusal one more time," she replied. Maybe there wasn't anything she could do, but she had to keep trying. If they wanted her gone, they'd have to drag her out.

An unfamiliar voice called through from the transporter room, presumably another of Almanza's people. "Lieutenant, someone's coming through. A Commander Kirk, from the *U.S.S. Mizuki*? He said his presence was requested. He's . . . ah, he's on his way, sir."

Carol's stomach unknotted, not entirely but enough for her to breathe.

"Who authorized this?" Almanza asked, turning to one of his engineers. Carol tuned out their conversation, watching the lab entry. In another beat, Jim walked through, and in spite of the circumstances, Carol couldn't help a moment of something like awe at the sight of him. The gentle, smiling man she had come to love was the picture of authority, his shoulders back, his expression set. He looked like . . . like . . .

Like a Starfleet commander.

Almanza snapped to, saluting briskly. "Commander. I wasn't informed that anyone else would be coming."

Jim nodded at him, at the engineers who were still rising to their feet. "As you were. I was asked to act as liaison between Kraden's team and ours. I have a prior relationship to Doctor Marcus, and it was thought that I could be helpful in coordinating your efforts here."

Almanza nodded. "Yes, sir."

"Report?"

The two men stepped away from Carol, the lieutenant launching into an update of the situation. It didn't take him long to paint the grim picture, but at the conclusion, Jim actually smiled. The expression was somehow authoritative and charming at the same time.

"I don't want to step on your toes, Lieutenant," he said, raising his voice slightly so that Carol could hear. "It sounds like you're handling the force field situation appropriately. I'll talk with the doctor and we'll see what we can do about organizing the security check."

If he'd had any lingering doubts about Jim's presence, the smile undid them. Almanza smiled back, gave a brisk nod before moving off to join his engineering team. Jim waited a beat, then hurried over to Carol. Even that seemed official, a strong, confident, natural stride—until he reached her. As soon as their eyes met, she could see the compassion and concern in him, the softness that he'd hidden from Almanza.

No, not hidden. And not softness. He was only being himself, rising to whatever the occasion demanded.

"What do you need me to do, Carol?" His voice was sure but infinitely gentle.

"Keep me out of lockup, for one," she said. "And get my people out of it."

"Done," Jim said. "They'll . . . you'll all have to be supervised in here, though. I'm sorry, but until the sabotage questions are answered—"

Carol nodded. She'd expected as much. "That's fine. If we can get a line on enough of a compound called phelistium, we might be able to fix all of . . . of that." She motioned vaguely at the window overlooking the test plot, suddenly blinking back tears. She wanted very much for Jim to touch her, to hold her but knew that he couldn't. Not here, not now.

He's who he wants to be, she thought, the thought a random one, the timing all wrong. *Who he* needs *to be.*

"Carol," he began, but she shook her head. She couldn't afford to fall to pieces, and an embrace from Jim would be all it took.

"Once we get the phelistium, we can work the numbers on our neutralizing compound," she said. "If you could keep your friends focused on extending that force field, it would keep them out of our way."

"They're here to help, Carol," Jim said. "We all are."

She still felt like crying but felt a flash of anger at the near hurt in his tone. As though she were being unreasonable, after Starfleet had barged in and taken over. It wasn't that he was wrong, exactly, but that awareness didn't help matters.

Not time to argue.

"Of course," she said. "Thank you. Tell them that I'll release access to whatever research materials they want to see. And that we'll all cooperate with their investigation as soon as Inception is neutralized."

He nodded, gave her a look of such warm assurance that it almost *was* an embrace, and then broke away to join his colleagues.

Relieved somewhat, Carol checked with Dachmes—Inception had progressed another three centimeters—and then Mac, who had an idea. He had a contact at a nearby starbase who had access to several databases that documented chemical storage facilities all over the galaxy.

"He can't get direct access to the phelistium, but he should be able to tell us who can," Mac said.

It was an added delay, having to go through

a middleman. They'd have to make additional contacts and deal with transport. The chance that they could neutralize Inception before it effected a fault line seemed to keep dropping. On the other hand, if they could get all they needed in a single shipment, that could save them some time. Carol forced herself to concentrate, to make the best of it.

"Call him," she said. "I'll get the others. We can have everything standing by."

With a last, lingering look at her beloved—he stood with his back to her, his arms folded, seemingly as unaware of her presence as she was of his—she headed for the back hall. She had just reached the common room when Leila hurried around a corner, almost knocking into her.

"My friend called," Leila said. Her expression was almost frantic, a padd clutched in one hand. She took a deep breath.

"I thought you were in the common room," Carol said.

Leila nodded. "They're still letting us do research, though, and I had to get my notes. My friend, my . . . my officer contacted me, with an idea. J.C. and Eric both think it will work. I do too. But we're going to need someone from Starfleet to help us, someone who can access a starship."

Leila's excitement was palpable, and contagious. Carol felt a rush of hope, pure and light, run through her.

"That shouldn't be a problem at all," she said.

Kent was having trouble pulling himself together. He'd gone to Redpeace headquarters after the press conference, enjoyed the buoyant atmosphere and eager chatter from the online watchers for a while before retiring to his office to work on their next statement. The next conference would take place directly in front of their office in a few moments, backdropped by the stark beauty of Ascraeus Mons, the northernmost mountain in Tharsis Montes. The timing, the setting, everything was perfect, but the few phrases he'd written so far were clumsy and redundant, as subtle as a rock to the head. Each time he tried to settle into the task, to choose the words that would inspire, all he could think of, all he could *see* was the look on the face of that man from the press conference, his frantic words drowning out the sounds of Kent's own thoughts.

There's too much nitrilin.

What would it mean if the solution breached the force field? He didn't know, didn't know enough about the experiment's specifics. But he knew that the compound Marcus had been dabbling with was some kind of an explosive. The scientists might be in danger, but they could always run away, get away. People could be evacuated; they could choose to leave. Beyond that, *Mars* could be in some kind of danger. The planet that he had sworn to try to protect.

His monitor chirped and he answered the call in a daze.

"Kent?" The voice was a half whisper, disguised by a rudimentary pitch-distortion device, the face onscreen cloaked in darkness.

"Yes. Who is this?" He checked the incoming signal, but the origin was blocked.

"I just want to warn you. Kraden is trying to cover up what's happening at that lab, but there's a possibility . . . there's a chance that things are getting worse. You should think about moving camp."

Kent blinked. It was Josh Swanson, he was certain of it despite the shadows, the artificial tinniness of the voice. He instinctively dropped his own voice to an indignant whisper. "What do you think you're doing, contacting me here?"

"There's no tracer on my signal, don't worry. Just do what I'm telling you. Listen, you have to believe me—it wasn't supposed to happen like this. Something went wrong, but it's not my fault."

Kent felt his face heating up. "I'm not interested in whose fault it was. If there's danger here, the colonists need to know."

There was a glimmer of smirk from the darkness. *"Oh, really? Who's going to tell them? You?"*

Kent was momentarily speechless. When he found his voice, it was subdued. "What kind of danger are we talking about? How long?"

"I don't know. My contact got a message out just after things started happening, but that was a while ago."

"This is from your friend at the lab?"

Swanson nodded, did his best to sound appropriately furtive. *"My* contact. *Word has it there's a significant possibility of a . . . seismic event."*

Kent felt a prickling tightness across his chest. "You mean a quake."

"Whatever you want to call it, you should get your people out. My contact says it could be a big one. Their solution has infected all the soil below it, and seismic activity will probably make it spread even farther."

"But isn't Starfleet there?" Kent asked. "Why haven't they notified the colonists?"

Swanson snorted. *"Because they think they can fix this before it gets any worse. Because they're arrogant, and they're unethical. Like I have to tell you."*

Arrogant and unethical. Had he ever been so blindly hypocritical? He wrestled with his anger—at Swanson, at himself—and finally managed to find his voice again. "We have to do something."

"That's up to you, if you don't mind implicating yourself. Look, I have to go. I suggest you do the same."

The monitor went blank. Kent continued to stare at the dead screen, paralyzed.

I didn't know, Jess. He could see her face so clearly in his mind's eye, it was as though she were actually on the monitor. He could see the disappointment on her face, the sadness—and the fury. Consorting with criminals like Swanson—what could he have been thinking? How could this disaster ever be justified, even if the unthinkable didn't happen?

Perhaps Swanson was wrong, or misinformed. He'd said himself that his information wasn't current. And Starfleet was trained to deal with this kind of thing. If they couldn't bring things under control, they would evacuate. They probably had a handle on the situation already. Kent could only hope. The irony of placing his trust in Starfleet was not lost on him, and it was proving as bitter as he might have expected.

Jess, I thought I was doing the best thing. I thought I had no other choice. I wanted it so badly . . . He remembered the press conference earlier, remembered how he'd determined to lay Redpeace's success at the foot of his lost wife's grave, and felt a knot form in his throat. *Not like this.*

His monitor chirped, signaling another call.

Kent tapped at the keys, his memory of Jess's face disappearing in a blur of pixels.

It was one of their volunteers, in the outer office. A dark-haired young woman, Merle something, called in to help with the expected flux of netsite calls. Her cheeks sparkled with applied glitter.

"Mister Kent, are you ready for your statement?"

"I . . . yes, just one moment please. I'll be . . ." His voice was faint, distracted. He realized, with horror, that his eyes were wet. "I'll be right there."

"The correspondents are here."

"Yes, I'll be there in a moment."

Merle something hesitated, then flashed him a beaming smile. For the barest flicker of a second, he saw Jess in her, in her eyes.

"I just wanted to say, I'm so happy to be here today. Things are really happening, you know? My family's been on Mars for three generations now, and it feels great to be involved, keeping it red, you know? You must be proud of what you've done here."

Kent had nothing to say to her. He stared at the hopeful, optimistic young woman and found no words. Her smile finally faltered slightly.

"Well, then, I'll let them know you're on your way," she said, and tapped a key.

Kent slumped, the tears spilling out. The shame, the self-loathing, the profound sense of betrayal to who he once was washed over him like an ocean. He couldn't afford to lose it like this, not now. This might be his one chance to broadcast the message to an audience of billions, but as the tears came faster, he knew that he was not going to be the one to deliver it. He didn't deserve to be.

It took several calls and more than a few favors promised, but as Kirk settled into the captain's seat of the *U.S.S. Aloia,* he felt certain that it had been worth the effort. The bridge, spacious and gleaming, looked good from where he was sitting; the controls felt right under his fingers, as though the chair had been designed with him in mind. He'd handled the much smaller *Mizuki,* of course, and even the *Farragut* once or twice, under Captain Garrovick's watchful eye, but this turn at *Aloia*'s conn, as captain and ranking officer on a mission of paramount importance to the safety and well-being of millions of Martian citizens . . . In spite of the circumstances, he couldn't help a feeling of intense satisfaction.

If it actually works, all the better, he thought lightly, although there was nothing humorous about the situation. It had to work. Besides the danger to Mars and its people, Carol's career would be over if it didn't. He felt another flush of rage at Whole Earth's sabotage but quickly set it aside. Command, he'd learned through the years, was to some extent about maintaining control of oneself. Sometimes, it was the only thing one *could* control.

Carol believed she'd found a way to stop the spread of the Inception process, and she needed a starship to do it, along with a high-density force field projector. With a nod of approval from Almanza, now manning the projector just beamed to the lab—and a word or two in the appropriate ear from Captain Olin—Starfleet Command had approved the idea and offered use of the *Aloia*. The *Aloia* was a ship without a crew, a brand-new *Miranda*-class that had been in dry dock at Utopia Planitia for a month or so, awaiting assignment. Awaiting a captain. Of course, this operation would take only a few hours at the very most, and she harbored less than a skeleton crew, all culled from the station. Half weren't even on active duty, had come from other ships being repaired or refitted. Still, this was an experience he would not be likely to forget.

Kirk nodded to his helm officer. "I'll ask you to maneuver her carefully. I don't intend for her new captain to have any complaints about the way she's been handled."

The officer nodded solemnly. "Of course,

Commander. No one will know we even took her out."

Kirk smiled. "I have no doubt. At your leave, Mister."

The impulse engines hummed, and the ship gently slid from the docking ring, turning so that the vast blank of space spun across the view screen before Mars came up, a dusky red half sphere beneath them. Kirk gave the few directions that were necessary, bringing the *Aloia* into a close orbit that would pass directly over Kraden's lab. It didn't take long.

"We're approaching, Commander."

Kirk tapped the control panel beneath his right hand, alerting sciences. "Begin measurement of substrata. Coordinate with engineering on transporter capacity and tractor beam range."

"Aye, sir."

He listened attentively to the conversation between the chief engineer, a Mister Young, and the "senior" science officer, a second lieutenant called Grathe. They exchanged information, hammering out the details. If it worked, it would be the first undertaking of its kind, at least that Kirk had ever heard about. When the two men were finally in agreement on the numbers, Kirk stepped in once more, told them to stand by.

"Do we have contact with the lab?" he asked.

The communications officer stood vigil at her blinking board. "Yes, Commander."

"Tell them we're ready to begin. Transporters, lock on."

Young answered him from the transporter room. *"Locked on, sir."*

The communications officer pressed her finger to her ear receiver. "They're giving us the go-ahead, sir. Lieutenant Almanza says the field is ready and is standing by for direction."

Kirk nodded, took a breath. "Let's beam it up, gentlemen."

With Almanza, Grathe, and Young all in verbal contact, the ship's transporters began the process of removing a wafer-thin slice of frozen Martian substrata, approximately one kilometer beneath the test plot. It would be brought up in pieces, held in carrier wave, and finally be "stacked" within a tractor beam field. Almanza was standing by to project the force field, laying it across the substrata acreage as each section was beamed out. The "floor" field would intersect with the descending "wall" fields, containing the Inception process entirely.

Kirk let the men work, listened as they carefully applied their skills to the task at hand. The project unfolded with barely a hitch: the force field spread out beneath the test plot as Grathe and Young beamed the thin cross section of matter from the ground. The rock being taken out was micromillimeters thick, just enough to allow for the force field. There were a few false starts, and twice Almanza's team wasn't able to get the field projected in time; a second layer had to be removed. Both times Kirk and the others waited in tense silence to hear from Alison Simhbib, Carol's Martian geologist. And both times she was able to tell them that the settling had been minor.

Finally, Young called out that the last assigned plot was locked on, and a moment later, Almanza confirmed that the force field "box" was complete. Seconds later, engineering informed the bridge that the tractor beam's load was stable, nearly a half ton of frozen Martian rock suspended behind the *Aloia*. Kirk couldn't help a grin.

We did it, Carol. He could only hope that she had been able to locate the proper chemicals to neutralize the ruined solution.

The communications officer was also smiling. "Doctor Marcus confirms containment of Inception process. She sends her thanks."

Kirk nodded. "Tell her that it was our pleasure. Helm, set course for Titan, full impulse."

Geologists were standing by at the Starfleet facility on Saturn's largest moon to receive the chunk of Martian subterranean rock. Once the *Aloia* delivered it, she would return to Utopia Planitia, her temporary crew disbanded. He could be back at the Kraden lab in another two or three hours, if all went smoothly. He expected that it would.

"Course set, Commander."

Kirk leaned back in the chair, *his* chair, relaxing for the first time since he'd first heard the news about Inception. He hoped that Carol would see, in spite of her misgivings, how effective, how *crucial* Starfleet could be in times of crisis. Perhaps she would even reconsider a few things, about what she wanted in her own future. He'd been so afraid when he hadn't been able to get through to her, it had made him rethink a few things himself. He was willing to give up almost anything to keep her, he'd decided. He let his hands rest on the command chair's arms. Almost.

"Steady as she goes," he said, and the *Aloia* swung away from Mars, faced out into the bright blackness of space.

Thirteen

Lieutenant Almanza nodded to one of his engineers, who tapped at the controls of the projector, frowning. A second later, he looked up—and smiled.

"Force field intersection is holding," he said.

Almanza's team let out a cheer, the engineers grinning, the lieutenant clapping his men on their backs. Carol managed a smile, but most of her attention—and the attention of everyone on her team—was still riveted to Richard Dachmes, sitting at the mainframe. He tapped keys and called up lines of code as J.C. sent him the numbers from the reads. J.C., seated at a monitor farther down the counter, tapped keys of his own, the last tap an exaggerated punch at the data entry control.

"Atmospheric measurements are in," J.C. said.

The analysis came seconds later. "Collated," Dachmes said. "Gases-to-particle ratio says Inception process is contained."

Carol exhaled with relief. The force field would hold the atmospheric umbrella created by

Inception, even if all the soil was processed. They still needed to neutralize it, but Mars was safe.

Everyone cheered. Carol thanked Lieutenant Almanza and asked him to send her personal thanks to Commander Kirk. Almanza shook her hand warmly—but told her a beat later that his security people would want to start questioning her teammates as soon as they became available.

An incoming call to Mac was almost lost amid the relieved chatter of the scientists and engineers. He took it at the far corner of the lab. Carol watched closely, felt her hopes leap at the look that crossed his face. He waved her over a moment later.

"There's a company off Io that has a stock of phelistium," he said. "Two hundred micrograms. It can be here within the hour."

Carol nodded, her anxiety level slipping down several more notches. While Almanza and his men had been calibrating the force field projector, she'd had Dachmes and J.C. running simulations with their formulation to neutralize Inception. With the stocks of aleuthian gas already prepped, two hundred micrograms of phelistium was all they needed.

Dealing with Starfleet, dealing with Kraden—compared to what might have happened, to what very nearly did—those were minor headaches. Carol looked for a chair, her knees suddenly weak, and sat down smiling. It was over.

Everything went quickly after the phelistium arrived, and Almanza's security people started pulling the scientists out for questioning even as the process was being neutralized. Leila had just heard the final, positive results when she was tapped. After exchanging grins with Carol and the others still in the lab, she'd headed for the common room.

She sat on a padded bench, waiting to be called. When she'd arrived, Alison Simhbib had been in the same spot, but the geologist had been beckoned out a moment later by a handsome young security guard with a serious countenance, leaving Leila alone. She folded and unfolded her hands, wondering what they would ask her. She'd tell them whatever she knew, of course, but doubted very much that she'd have anything useful to contribute. What she knew about sabotage was . . . well, nothing. She thought perhaps the word was French.

She was still in a kind of shock, she thought, from everything that had happened. They all were, she was sure, but the shock was a warm one, considering the source of their salvation. Mister Spock's brilliant suggestion had rescued them from certain disaster. She hoped he was watching the net links, or had learned of the successful containment through Starfleet channels. She hadn't had an opportunity to call him back, and it didn't appear that she'd have a spare moment anytime soon. Carol wanted her to run an analysis of the Inception regolith as soon as she was done with her questioning, and after that—no one knew. Carol thought they'd be sent back to Earth, pending a full investigation of the matter by Starfleet and Kraden.

The door opened. Leila tensed slightly, but it was Tamara Irwin, not Starfleet. The shy girl—she was Leila's age but seemed younger to Leila, somehow—moved across the room, taking a seat next to her on the bench. She didn't speak. Her dark eyes were downcast, her face pale and pinched.

Leila felt a rush of compassion for the awkward scientist. She smiled at her, but Tam wouldn't look up.

"Tam, about the inventory," Leila said gently. "It was a mistake, but everyone makes mistakes. Considering how everything worked out, I'm sure no one will blame you."

Tam nodded, seemed to hunch tighter into herself.

"What happened here wasn't your fault," she

added, and she saw with some surprise that Tamara had begun to cry behind her fall of dark hair, tears slipping down her cheeks. When she spoke, her voice was a hoarse whisper.

"He said he loved me," she said.

"Who—" Leila began, and faltered, the implications forming. Tamara didn't seem to notice, tears rolling off the tip of her snubnose, falling into her lap.

"I had him meet me the day before we left," she said, "when I knew I'd be the only one in the lab. He didn't tell me he was going to tamper with the solution, he just said"—she took a deep, shuddering breath, struggling to get it out—"he just said he was going to do something to the equipment. I was doing the last inventory on the stores, and he asked me to leave for a minute, he said he wanted to make sure that I wouldn't be, that I wouldn't be *implicated*."

The young woman wailed, her head dropping even lower. She managed to repeat that he said he'd loved her before her words were entirely lost, her body racked with sobs. Leila automatically slid closer to her, slipped an arm around her shoulders as she cried. As dismaying, as *surprising* as her confession was, Leila couldn't help feeling sorry for her. Whatever she'd involved herself with, she was paying for it. Leila whispered vague assurances, patting Tam's back as she cried.

A few minutes later, when the security crewman opened the door and nodded to Leila, it was Tam who stood up. She wiped at her eyes, her face red and streaked, but managed a very small smile for Leila.

"I was stupid," she said, "but I might be able to fix at least some of it."

"No one was hurt, Tam," Leila said, but they both knew it wasn't so. Leila felt a stab of rage for the man who'd so manipulated the shy physicist, who'd almost certainly scarred her permanently. Whatever Starfleet would do to her, Leila had no doubt that it would be nothing to what "he" had done.

Tam nodded anyway and walked unsteadily across the room to meet her fate.

Kent materialized at the pad in the laboratory's airlock, took a deep breath as he looked around, tried to still the pounding of his heart. He hadn't spoken to the press since his minor breakdown, calling Don Byers to fill in for him back at Redpeace. But when Kraden decided to hold the latest press conference here—had, in fact, *invited* him to attend, along with a handful of proviro Martian politicians, presumably to demonstrate to the public that the lab was finally secure—he couldn't pass on the opportunity. He'd pulled himself together and made the trip.

"I'm here for the press conference," he said, and the engineer at the transporter controls nodded.

"Yes, sir. They're meeting in the main lock, just north of here. Let me call for an escort—"

"That won't be necessary," Kent said quickly. "Thank you."

Before the crewman could protest, Kent had hurried through the nearest exit. The north-south corridor outside presumably led directly to the conference room. Kent promptly turned south, seeking the lab. There was a chance that everyone had already assembled for the conference, but he hoped not; he wanted to speak to Carol Marcus personally. In the few hours since the links had reported Starfleet's assurances that all was well, meeting with Doctor Marcus had formed into something like an obsession for him. He wanted to know—he *needed* to know— if she had changed her mind about the nature of her work. The rational, reasonable part of him knew that it didn't really matter, that it had nothing to do with Redpeace's continuing mission or his own personal culpability in what had occurred, but there was another part of him that felt a kind of blind, grasping hope, that after experiencing the horror of the possible consequences of her actions, she might have learned something.

As though that would make it all okay, Jess said.

Kent shook away the thought, started checking doors for the lab entrance. He found a small common room and a restroom, and was about to try a branching corridor when he saw her approaching from the south, turning the corner with a Starfleet officer at her side. A commander, judging by the stripes on his sleeve, and familiar somehow.

Kirk. Kent recognized him as the couple approached. *From the summit.* The coincidence was startling, but it was fitting, somehow, that he would be here too. Kent straightened his shoulders, ready to meet them. Ready to convince them.

And maybe convince yourself? Jess whispered.

The couple stopped in front of him. Kirk's face registered a hint of surprise, there and gone in an instant. "Mister Kent," he said. "You must be lost. Do you need an escort to the press conference?"

"Commander," Kent said, nodding politely, "I was hoping to have a few words with the doctor—"

Kirk started to say something, but Carol waved him off.

"What is it, Mister Kent?" She addressed him coolly. She looked tired, bone-weary, in fact, but she carried herself with dignity.

"Doctor Marcus, I thought that perhaps . . . I was hoping that you might have reconsidered your stance on the type of experimentation that Kraden was doing here today," he said.

Her expression gave him nothing. "Why, Mister Kent? Have you?"

He shook his head, found the words that he'd spent a lifetime working toward achieving, believing them as he spoke. "My organization believes that Mars, like all planets, exists in its natural state for a reason, and that it is inherently wrong to manipulate and possibly cause irreversible damage to its ecosystem. Surely what happened here today must have shown you that."

Carol Marcus inhaled deeply before speaking. "Mister Kent, I understand what your motivation is. I understand that you are passionate about your cause, and I apologize for any insensitivity I may have shown you before, back at the station. But I do not agree with you, and neither does most of the galaxy."

"But it doesn't have to be that way," Kent

insisted. "People simply don't understand the effects of their behavior, and of experiments like yours. As a scientist, doesn't it upset you that this incident has irreparably damaged hundreds of square meters of Martian terrain? Terrain that can never be studied now in its natural state."

Kirk broke in. "Her researchers had nothing to do with that. Whole Earth—this Josh Swanson person, apparently—is the responsible party. You should be discussing this with him."

Kent managed to keep his head up, his gaze steady. "You're not wrong, Commander, but there's more to my side of the argument. You must try to understand my ideology—that natural resources have an intrinsic value that goes beyond their usefulness in consumption. Cut it down, use it up, throw it away. That's the attitude that must be changed."

"I think you're grossly overstating your case," Kirk said. "Starfleet and the Federation strive to preserve and reuse resources. Within the UFP, Terrans rank among the most environmentally conscious. If you compared our waste output now with that of a century ago, you'd have to be a Vulcan not to be impressed."

"I am impressed, but I believe that even stricter specifications are in order. I want to strive for sustainability—"

"We're on the same page, then, Mister Kent," Doctor Marcus interrupted. "I believe in sustainability as well, which is why my research is dedicated to ending universal hunger. I want every culture to be able to care for itself."

"It's a fine ideal, Doctor Marcus, but the effects of your experimentation serve only *people,*" Kent continued doggedly. "Don't you believe that, as intelligent beings, we have a responsibility to protect all life-forms? All environments?"

"I think most reasonable people want that," Kirk said. "But sometimes it doesn't work out that way, despite our best efforts. We can only do our best. And as intelligent beings, we can work toward prioritizing what's important—to all of us."

" 'All of us,' " Kent snapped. He'd wanted to talk to Carol Marcus, not this Starfleet poster boy. "Except the Martians. Why didn't Starfleet warn the colonists about what could have happened if the corrupted solution had reached the fault line?"

Kirk started to answer him and then stopped. "How did you know about that, Mister Kent? That information wasn't broadcast."

Kent hesitated, then fumbled out an answer. "There's information everywhere, if you know where to look for it. Redpeace is an environmental organization devoted to protecting Mars, if you weren't aware; we have some idea of her geology."

Kirk regarded him for an uncomfortable moment before speaking. "Not that you're owed an explanation, sir, but Starfleet was following procedure. A premature announcement might have created panic. It was deemed appropriate to postpone notification until we had made every effort to contain the incident."

He sounded so reasonable, so sure of himself. Kent struggled for a response—hadn't he spent his life finding ways to steer around such bland but poisonous rhetoric?—and could think of nothing. Anything he said would be so riddled with hypocrisy, he doubted he'd be able to choke it out. Instead, he turned back to Carol Marcus. She was why he'd come.

So talk to her, Jess said. *Really talk. Enough with the company line, my darling; make the connection.*

He cleared his throat and tried again. "Doctor, progress can hurt people. It can kill. Do you really want to end up responsible for some innocent's death, a tragedy that could have been prevented if only someone had taken a bit more care?"

"Of course not," Carol said. "We should all take care, Mister Kent, in everything we do. And when the unthinkable happens, when someone dies in the name of some impersonal cause, some great stride forward by the many, it makes no difference to the people who loved that person. Maybe they try to make it have some greater meaning, to give their loved one's death a purpose, to make his or her life worth something. But to me, life's value is measured in the people it touches. And trying to turn a careless, terrible accident into a cause . . ."

She shook her head, met his gaze squarely. "I'm sorry, Mister Kent. It's presumptuous of me to assume anything about you or your life. I'd like to say that what happened here wasn't my fault, but in truth, if I'd taken more care, I might have been able to prevent it. All I can do is try and learn from my own mistakes. And be grateful that no one was hurt here today."

Kent was stunned by her willingness to take responsibility. He felt lost, suddenly, his reasons for coming here unclear. If he'd wanted to absolve himself of guilt, she'd just made it exponentially worse by laying it across her own shoulders.

Confused and angry, he turned abruptly and began to walk down the hall, heading for the press conference, thinking that perhaps he wouldn't attend at all. He could call Don, get him to fill in again.

I shouldn't have come here, he thought. Jess remained conspicuously silent.

"Have a nice day, Mister Kent," Kirk called after him. The commander's tone was hard to read, but Kent thought he detected a mocking note in his voice. Considering his reasons for traveling to the lab, he thought there was a good chance that he deserved it.

Fourteen

Repperton had been smiling for a moment too long, but Carol couldn't quite bring herself to urge him to continue. She clenched and unclenched her hands beneath her desk, waiting for the hammer to drop. From Repperton's cues, it was inevitable.

She'd wanted to put off the call, wanted to leave it alone until she'd found her equilibrium, but considering all that had happened, she thought that might take a while. And most of her team had displayed such loyalty. She'd been pulled aside by almost everyone before they'd even left Mars, each expressing a desire to continue with the work. She owed it to them to call Kraden as quickly as possible. Upon returning to Earth, they'd immediately transported to the university lab. She was in her tiny office now, one floor up from the lab, where her team waited for word. Now, staring at Repperton's smug face, she wished she hadn't been in such a hurry.

"Yes, the preliminary stages did *show a great deal*

of promise," he finally said. *"Your initial testing was even more productive than we had hoped."*

She didn't have to wonder what he would say next. Still, she had to try and salvage what she could.

"Mister Repperton, I'd like to think that Kraden would base their decision on the science. You saw the first-run results. If not for the sabotage, Inception would have worked perfectly."

"That may be true." His smile was gone now. *"But considering all the bad publicity we've had to endure, I'm sure you'll understand why we cannot continue to fund your endeavor."*

It was what she'd expected. "The public's memory is short," Carol said. "Perhaps in a year or so—"

"The public's memory is indeed short, Doctor Marcus, for small-scale scandals and political blunders, things that don't involve the personal safety of Federation colonists." Repperton had rehearsed this, no doubt. *"I believe that this is one event that will stay fresh in the minds of many for years to come, even after they've forgotten what actually transpired. All they'll remember was that Kraden funded an experiment that very nearly caused a catastrophe on Mars, never mind who was actually responsible. Our board has made the decision to stay away from Mars for a while. A long while."*

"We could move to a DS lab—"

His smile was anything but friendly. *"Considering the judgment you displayed in dealing with our public relations department, Doctor, I'm sure you'll understand why Kraden has also elected to distance ourselves from you, for the time being. Not to mention your less than stringent criteria for selecting your team members."*

Carol's fists unclenched. *Well, that's that,* she thought. Never mind that Starfleet had already cleared her of negligence; she couldn't argue with Repperton's read of the situation. Kraden would be remembered as the perpetrator of the incident, and to some degree, that was her fault. "I understand," she said.

"Even if I personally *wanted to fund your project, this is a board decision,"* he added. *"And it is a final one."*

Carol nodded, made herself smile. The absurdity of these little societal norms were never more obvious than at times like these, but you couldn't risk burning bridges.

"Thank you for your time, Mister Repperton," she said, tapping at the monitor's controls before anything else could slip out.

Thank you for rubbing it in, just a little bit more.

Carol let herself cry for a moment, mourning Inception. It wasn't entirely unexpected, but she'd still hoped, anyway. The data from the initial test runs was all over the links, her work being praised in spite of what had almost happened. She'd thought that Kraden might choose to take a stand. But she was young and dispensable, an unknown scientist with no serious credentials, working with a team of amateurs.

The tears finally dried but stayed close. She'd been tearing up every other minute, it seemed, since . . . since she'd become pregnant, she supposed. It didn't help that she would say goodbye to Jim tomorrow, perhaps for the last time. And she still hadn't told him the reason it was going to be so difficult. She still hadn't told him that he was going to have a son, and she was fairly certain that she wouldn't, not now. All of her promises to herself, that talk she'd had with Leila—when he'd come to the lab, when he'd stepped in to help her, she'd seen the real Jim Kirk and had realized the truth of him.

Commander *Kirk. And he'll be a captain, soon enough. An admiral, someday, if he wants it.* It was his very essence, it was what he loved to do. He was meant to fly around the galaxy, commanding his ship, negotiating with exotic life-forms. Carol had no doubt that he would give it all up for a child, for their child. She just didn't want to be the one to ask him to. She wiped her face, tried to shake away the resentment. It wasn't his fault, not really. Being a father . . . She just didn't see it for him. Didn't see it *in* him. It was a big decision, but she thought it was the right one. For now, at least.

She took a few more moments to collect herself and then stood, steeling herself for what lay ahead. She had a lot of equipment to unpack and a team of good people waiting to hear that they were out of a job.

Leila was somehow surprised to find her apartment just as she had left it. Of course, she hadn't been gone long, and now that she lived by herself, there was no reason for anything to have been disturbed. Still, it felt as though an entire lifetime had passed since she had seen this room. She set her traveling cases on the floor near her bed and went straight to her computer.

She checked her messages quickly, her heart sinking a little as she realized that Mister Spock hadn't tried to contact her. She'd tried to contact him several times before leaving Mars, but he'd been unavailable. Finally, she'd nerved herself and left a brief message, asking him to call.

Leila sat down and leisurely browsed through her messages, looking at various net links that some of her colleagues had passed along. She was tired, still recovering from the adrenaline binge of Inception, but it was early. Besides, she wanted the distraction—from Carol's news about Kraden, mostly, but also from being alone. She was still getting used to living by herself, and wishing she could see Mister Spock didn't help. His ship was surely still in dock, but he'd made it clear that he'd had no plans to return to Earth. It might be a while before they could meet again face-to-face. An article about biosynthetic pathways caught her eye, but she couldn't focus on it. She marked it for later and switched off her monitor, deciding she might go to sleep early after all. Even after hearing that they were no longer a team, J.C. and Mac and the others had all pitched in to help Carol get the equipment unloaded. Trying to unpack all of it before nightfall had been daunting—not to mention depressing— and much of the work had been left for the following day. Leila meant to go back to help, so she might as well get enough rest.

There was still plenty of coverage about the experiment, but she'd had enough of it for now. Josh Swanson, Whole Earth's "masked man," had been caught, thanks to Tamara Irwin's tip-off; two of his accomplices were also being held. Tam was going to have to spend some time in a low-security facility, but at least she'd been cooperative enough to spare herself a worse fate. Even though she'd caused a lot of trouble for Carol, for all of them, Leila still felt bad for her. As strange as it seemed, she hadn't meant any harm. She'd simply had the misfortune to fall in love with a man who only wanted to use her, and she had been too naïve to see it. Leila thought it must have been terribly difficult for her to turn her lover in, considering that she obviously still felt something for him.

Whole Earth's tampering had been so ill conceived it was being called a miracle that nobody had been hurt. From the press reports, it seemed that they hadn't really had a coherent plan. Three of the activists had simply blundered into the university lab and messed with everything they could get their hands on. All three of them were now busily pointing fingers at each other, insisting that their own part in the sabotage had been minor.

Of course, Leila knew it was hardly a miracle that the colonies had been saved. Mister Spock's simple and ingenious idea—facilitating the insertion of an industrial force field by use of a starship's transporters—had been responsible. Perhaps Carol or one of the Starfleet engineers would have thought of something similar, eventually, but the pressure of the situation had been stressful, to say the least, perhaps clouding logic. It had taken a Vulcan mind to achieve the necessary clarity so quickly. She readied herself for bed and fell asleep thinking of him, wondering if she could ever hope to achieve such clarity.

Leila had been asleep for about a half an hour when she was awakened by the chime of her computer. Reluctant to get up, she asked the computer to identify the caller. When the mechanical voice spoke Mister Spock's name, she was on her feet in a flash, sitting in front of the computer and pushing her sleep-ruffled hair behind her ears before it could signal a second time. Her heart pounding, she answered the call, felt her stomach knot pleasantly at the sight of him.

"Hello, Mister Spock," she said.

"Miss Kalomi. I hope I'm not disturbing you."

"Not at all. It's . . . I'm very glad you've called."

"I received a message earlier that you wished to speak with me. I attempted to contact you at the Martian laboratory but received a signal informing me that you and the other scientists had returned to Earth. I regret that I was unable to contact you until now, but it can be difficult for me to take personal time away from my duties to devote to correspondence."

"It's quite all right, Mister Spock. I appreciate

that you would return my call in the first place. I know you must be busy. I only wanted to thank you for helping us. Your advice almost certainly saved thousands of lives."

One of his eyebrows arched. *"I did my duty, as a Starfleet officer and a scientist. It was only logical."*

"Yes, of course. Still, I'd like to thank you, on behalf of Doctor Marcus and the rest of the team."

Spock bowed his head to one side, an acceptance. She smiled at him. Although he hadn't specifically asked to remain anonymous, she hadn't given his name out to anyone, saying only that she'd received her information from a friend. Mister Spock was obviously an extremely private person.

"I am curious to know, Miss Kalomi, what the future course of action will be for your experiment."

Her smile faded. "I'm sorry to say that our experiment will not continue. Kraden has pulled their funding."

"That is regrettable. I believe your research would have yielded favorable results."

"I think so too."

He looked as though he meant to end the call, and Leila quickly tried to think of a means to extend the conversation.

"I must admit, I have missed our conversations since we parted last," she said.

Spock nodded once. *"Our time together was indeed stimulating."*

She felt suddenly bold. "Does that mean you miss them too?"

He gazed at her silently, apparently unsure how to reply. Leila searched for an appropriate follow-up, wanting to keep him a little longer.

"Mister Spock, I feel compelled to thank you again for what you did. I know I'm repeating myself, but I . . . I suppose it's just good to see your face again. I wish I could speak with you in person."

"Does the communicator restrict your ability to speak freely?"

"No, it doesn't, it's only a personal desire." She felt her face growing hot. She wanted so badly to tell him how she felt, but if she would only make a fool of herself—

"A personal desire?"

"Yes. Yes, you see, Terrans—if we care for someone, if we enjoy his or her company, it's more than just speaking, it's more than seeing one another every once in a while—"

"You speak of personal relationships between humans." Spock's tone was almost entirely inflectionless. *"Friendships."*

"Yes, friendships, but there's more than that. You told me that Vulcans marry, that they—" She shouldn't, she knew, but could not stop herself. "That they may prefer the company of one over another?"

"That is correct, although I believe the purpose differs from that of humans, as well as the criteria. Humans tend to form relationships based on emotion, rather than tradition, procreation, or intellectual compatibility."

"That isn't true," Leila said. "Many humans rely on tradition when they form relationships, and a great part of human love relies on intellectual compatibility."

Spock didn't respond, but the way he studied her, the searching expression of his gaze . . . She kept talking, not sure if he was simply curious or if it was something more.

"Don't you feel . . . don't you believe that you and I are compatible, intellectually?"

"You have a fine mind. As I've already stated, I found our conversations to be most stimulating."

"I feel stimulated by *you*. Intellectually and . . . otherwise."

He cocked his head slightly. *"In what way do you mean, Miss Kalomi?"*

Her pulse was pounding at her throat. "I mean that I love you, Mister Spock. I'm in love with you."

He did not respond right away, and in the few impossibly long seconds that passed, she knew that she had made a mistake. Even if he returned her feelings on any level—which she believed he did—he would never permit himself to acknowledge it. She felt a stone in her throat, in the pit of her stomach.

His frown, the tone of his voice when he spoke, suggested confusion. *"Miss Kalomi, I am not aware of an appropriate response to your declaration."*

Leila looked away. "I'm sorry."

"I would like to understand what you expect by your expressed sentiment. Please, Miss Kalomi. I do not wish to cause you any further . . . discomfort."

Leila smiled sadly. "Well, a human male, I suppose, would tell me . . . how *he* felt. Whether or not he loved me back."

"I see. In that case, Miss Kalomi, my response must be that I do not love you, as I am incapable of love."

She could not speak for her tears. She wanted to tell him that she didn't believe him, that he was not incapable of love, he had simply learned to ignore his emotions so long ago that he had forgotten what they were for. But maybe she was fooling herself. It was easy enough to believe him as he watched her cry, his expression as stoic, as ungiving as ever. Yet when she looked into his eyes, she could not let go of the certainty that there was still something there, something just for her.

It doesn't matter, though, does it? It never did.

"I should go," she managed. "Thank you for . . . for returning my call."

"It was not my intention to cause you distress. I feel it would be inappropriate for me to leave you in your current state."

She smiled slightly. In his way, he was asking her if she was all right before ending the call. Perhaps it was true that all men were alike, adhering to the same code that enabled them to break women's hearts all over the galaxy.

"I'll recover," she said, wondering as she said it if it was true. She knew, of course, that she would pick up and move on. But she also knew—she *knew*—that no other man would move her the way that this one had.

"Good-bye, Mister Spock. I will not forget you."

"Live long and prosper, Miss Kalomi," he said, and then he was gone.

Spock turned away from his monitor, contemplative. He could not fully comprehend why she had elected to reveal her feelings, understanding what she did of his Vulcan heritage. It was possible that his partly human ancestry had inspired in Leila Kalomi a belief that he was capable of returning her love. But considering their prior conversations regarding any aspect of the matter, he couldn't see how. It struck him as odd that she—that many species, actually—seemed to feel compelled to induce the subject of their desires to reciprocate those feelings. Odd, and in this particular instance, unfortunate.

Yearning, he thought, templing his fingers. *The desire to have what one has not.* Too often, it was not the desire to achieve knowledge, or spiritual completion; it was not a desire for possibilities within. This yearning, this desire that seemed to drive so much of the galaxy into paroxysms of unrest was the wish to obtain something *else*—land, or resources. Or love.

Had some part of him yearned for Miss Kalomi, for her company? Perhaps, in that he had, in fact, taken some pleasure in seeing her. But he had also taken pleasure in seeing some of the science and industry museums of Earth. Obviously, considering the variables in experience, they could not be compared.

His computer signaled. He touched the control. "Spock here."

It was the captain. *"I've called a senior officers' meeting in conference one, at fifteen hundred hours. I*

*want to go over the new scheduling rosters, and I'd like
your input."*

"Yes, Captain."

A glance at the monitor told him that he had
forty minutes until his presence was required.
He decided he would arrive early and spend the
spare time formulating possible shift changes.
He also decided, as he left his quarters, that he
would not seek any further contact with Leila
Kalomi. He expected, all things considered, that
she would elect to do the same.

Fifteen

Carol ate very little of her meal, although the food was excellent. The restaurant had been highly recommended by Doc Evans and was worthy of the praise. But as Kirk picked over his own pasta, he realized that the quality of the food wasn't actually the problem.

"Aren't you hungry?" he asked, nodding at her nearly full plate. The question was almost automatic, a polite inquiry in place of what he should say, what he knew he should ask. He didn't want to, though. She'd been distant with him since before Mars, but he still didn't want to talk about it, fully aware of what she was likely to say. Fully aware that he still didn't know what he wanted to do.

That's not true. You know, you just don't want to admit it. The thought was more honest than he wanted to acknowledge, even now. But his brief stint as the captain of the *U.S.S. Aloia* had clarified a lot of things for him.

"I guess not," she said, and sighed. Her smile was faint. "I've still got a lot of unpacking to do at the lab. And I guess . . . I guess I've been thinking that you're going to leave me again soon."

He pushed his plate aside, reached for one of her hands.

"I'm sorry," she said. "I know you've got almost a week left, but I don't think . . . I can't keep pretending—"

"Carol," he said softly, stroked her fingers. It hurt, worse than he'd expected, and although he knew what he wanted, knew where his future lay, he realized that he couldn't let it go. Couldn't let *her* go, not without at least trying. He loved her.

"Before you asked me to come to the lab, I thought about what it would mean to lose you," he said. "The thought of never seeing you again was like the end of the world."

A tear trickled down one of her golden cheekbones, in spite of her smile. She started to respond, but he grasped her hand tighter, squeezed her delicate fingers within his own.

"Don't say anything, Carol, not yet. I just wondered . . . I thought that maybe I could talk you into changing your mind."

"Changing my mind?"

"About Starfleet." He drew a deep breath. "I wondered what you would say if I asked you to—"

She released his hand. "Don't, please," she half whispered. Behind her tears, she was beautiful. Beautiful and merciful and deeply, terribly sad. "You already know what my answer would have to be."

His vague hopes crumbled, yet he felt a shameful glimmer of relief beneath his own sorrow. He did love her, as much as he'd ever loved anyone. But he couldn't ask her to give up her dreams for his, either. In a way, she'd released them both.

"Yes," he said, sitting back in his seat. "I know."

Karen Dupree turned to look at Kent, and he smiled at her. He'd been smiling a lot over the last few days, his decision having lifted a massive weight from his shoulders. She smiled back, turning again toward the podium, where Don Byers had finished delivering their quarterly report and was now going over their newly revised mission statement. Kent looked out into the audience of Terran Redpeace members and supporters, most of them hanging on every one of Byers's words. He'd become a good speaker over the years, engaging and entertaining. Kent would be up next; they were all expecting to hear his take on the Kraden debacle. It was their first Earth conference since the incident, held at their original headquarters. It was fitting that he'd be making his announcement here, not two klicks from where it had all started for him, where he and Jess had grown up together. There would be another conference on Mars in a few days, but he wouldn't be speaking there.

"We're putting a new face on Redpeace," Byers said. "We want to do whatever we can to keep our newfound visibility high, while simultaneously distancing ourselves from violent groups like Whole Earth. In the wake of this near tragedy, we want it made absolutely clear that our goals and methodology are entirely disparate from Whole Earth and groups like it."

The reception was wholeheartedly positive, their friends and colleagues, numerous members of the press—who, until the Mars incident, had never managed to attend one of the quarterly conferences—all clapping loudly for the well-spoken Byers. Don nodded his acceptance of it, then called Kent up with a brief but glowing introduction. The applause grew as Kent rose from his seat, as Don moved to sit back down just to the left of the podium. Kent hooked his friend's arm, kept him standing.

"Don't sit down just yet," he said.

Byers complied, puzzled, as Kent took his

place in front of the crowd. He felt their appreciative gazes, their enthusiasm and loyalty, and was warmed by it. The cause—not just for Mars, but for maintaining natural integrity throughout the galaxy—had never been so well supported or so public. He knew that great things would come of such loving attention, such fervent belief in the power of conservation.

"Friends and supporters, people of the press," Kent began, his voice carrying clear and strong, not a hint of hesitation. "I thank each and every one of you for your loyalty and support throughout my service as chairperson for the Immutable Foundation, also known as Redpeace." A few people chuckled, though most of the crowd was so accustomed to the nickname that it failed to rouse them.

"I can't tell you how much I've appreciated everything you've done for this organization," he continued, "from volunteering, to financial support, to just showing up whenever there was a press conference or a protest. You *are* this organization." Murmurs of approval went up all around him.

"What we do—what we try to do—is make a positive difference in this galaxy, to keep all of our worlds safe and sound for every living creature. And for generations to come." His voice broke slightly, and he cleared his throat before continuing. It was the right thing, he knew it, but that didn't mean it was painless.

"I love what we stand for," he said, smiling out at them all. "And so it is with the greatest regret that I must announce my resignation as chair, effective immediately."

"Thad—" Byers, standing to his side, clutched him by the forearm.

Kent waved him off. "I've chosen to step down for personal reasons, and I would like to be the first to nominate Don Byers as my replacement. Don?"

Byers appeared flabbergasted as the hall erupted into applause. Kent stepped away from the podium, fighting to contain himself as he took his seat.

"Well, I don't know what to say," Byers began, but then he launched into a smooth and competent acceptance speech, just as Kent had known he would. Don was the perfect man for this job. A much more capable and deserving man than Kent had ever been.

Kent did not meet the gaze of any of the other board members, sitting all around him, until the meeting had been adjourned and most of the crowd had trickled out. He did the expected obligatory round of hand shaking and embraces, carefully avoiding the questions, and finally it was over. He let out a deep breath and headed for the building's main exit. Don Byers caught up to him just before he reached it.

"Thad," Byers said, his face still flushed from all the excitement, his eyes sparkling, though he wasn't smiling. He wore an expression of sincere concern. "I still can't believe that you did this. No one can. I hope you know how much I appreciate that you would want to pass the baton to me—and I know you said your reasons were personal—but why?"

Kent considered, for a half second, actually telling him the truth. He'd known Don Byers for more than fifteen years, and if anyone deserved an explanation, it was Don. But what could he say? That he'd wavered when he shouldn't have? That in his desperation to give his own life meaning, he'd tried to cheat? He'd told himself, all these years, that it was for Jess, that it had all been for Jess, but the truth was he just hadn't ever gotten around to inventing a reason to live without her. What had happened at Tyn Sei, with the Immutable Foundation, Redpeace—they had all been ways to structure an anger that should have been laid to rest long ago. After his awkward and confusing meeting with Carol Marcus, he'd done a lot of thinking. And though he still believed in the work, he didn't want to be angry anymore. That anger had allowed him to set aside his common sense, to collaborate, even indirectly, with the likes of Josh Swanson, and then keep his mouth shut about it when he should have spoken up.

Perhaps, though, it wasn't so bad to go out with an ounce of integrity left, at least in an old friend's admiring gaze.

"It was time, Don," he said. "That's all."

Don hesitated, then nodded. "If you say so, Thad."

The two men shook hands and parted, Kent promising to keep in touch until Don got settled. As the new chair of Redpeace headed for the transporters, a lively spring in his step, Thad silently wished him well. He turned back to the main exit and stepped out into the sun-filled afternoon.

The sky was a brilliant blue, almost turquoise, and the freshness of the warm air filled him with renewed energy. He walked for more than a kilometer before he broke into a jog, caring not at all that he was sweating into his suit, that he must look quite strange to any passersby. It felt good to run, to be outside and free from responsibility. A half klick later, he hit an old dirt path that had never been paved, that he still remembered clearly from his childhood. He'd walked the path with Jess many times.

He ascended the narrow path to a broad expanse of unmowed green, settling back into a walk, letting himself cool off. Moments later, he saw the first of the markers that signified the old cemetery, then a second and third. The large, polished blocks of granite and plasticrete jutted up from the uneven terrain, the soil having settled many generations ago, when Terrans still buried their dead. He walked among the graves, headed roughly northwest. Birds sang randomly in the shadow-washed trees, a light wind blowing softly. He reached the glassed-in mausoleum and entered, low lights winking on as he opened the door.

How many years since he'd come here? He couldn't remember. At least ten. His footsteps echoed across the stone floor, and he ran his hands along the cool wall that bore the names of so many, some of them relatives or acquaintances of his ancestors, he was sure. Someday his name would be here too. His fingers came to rest on a name engraved just below his shoulder, and he bent slightly at the knees to press his cheek to it, to feel the chill stone against his face.

I haven't given up Jess, he silently promised. *I'll never give up. But you can rest now, my love, really*

*and truly. I swear, I won't let you down like that
again. Never again.*

There wasn't too much left to do by lunchtime
on the fourth day after their return, so following a final meal together, most of the Inception
team went their separate ways. The good-byes
were sad, though not overly so. In spite of what
they'd gone through together, they'd known
each other only a short time, really. And because
Leila had nowhere in particular she had to be,
she volunteered to go back to the lab with Carol,
to finish up.

She'd just unpacked the last of the sensor
packs when Carol joined her in storage, setting
a box of recalibrated tricorders on a low shelf.
Leila turned and smiled at her, pushing her hair
behind her ears.

"I think that's everything, Doctor," she said.

"I thought you were going to call me Carol
from now on," Carol said, smiling back. "And
I think you're right. Thank you for helping me
finish."

Leila shrugged. "I had nothing else to do."

Carol's smile faded. "I know. And again,
I'm so sorry about how things turned out with
Kraden. Maybe if I'd played ball a little better—"

"No, it's not that," Leila interrupted. "I just

meant . . . I meant I don't have anything to go home to at the moment. No one waiting."

She said it lightly, but something must have shown in her demeanor, her tone. Carol gave her a sympathetic smile, leaning back against one wall of shelves and folding her arms.

"Does that mean that your officer . . ."

Leila nodded. "It wasn't meant to happen, I suppose." She wanted to sound careless, but her heart wasn't in it. She wasn't ready for carelessness yet.

Carol nodded. "I see. Well, if it makes you feel any better, my Starfleet officer and I also parted ways. Just after we got back."

Perhaps she too was trying to be casual about it, but there was a tightness at the corners of her mouth that said otherwise. Leila nodded in turn, her expression solemn. She understood. They were silent for a moment, each, perhaps, lost in her own feelings of sorrow, of loss, but when their gazes met once more, both women smiled.

"It's not the end of the world, is it?" Carol asked.

"No, it's not," Leila agreed.

"We're intelligent, attractive, capable women, you and I, complete within ourselves. And we have a lot of life ahead of us. Lots of possibilities."

"That's right." Leila had been considering

that trip to the rain forest again, with Professor
Bonner's team. She would go, she decided suddenly, involve herself in a new project. It would
be fully involving too—the workload was heavy,
and there would be no transporters or modern
conveniences for kilometers around; one had to
rely on small craft to get from place to place. It
would be like living in the twenty-second century, and just the thought of it was suddenly
quite appealing to her. "A universe full."

They locked up the storage room and started
for the transporters, both walking slowly.

"So then," said Carol, "what's next for you,
do you think?"

"Travel." Leila told Carol a little about Professor Bonner's trip, the doctor listening ap-
provingly.

"What about you?" Leila asked, as they
reached the transporter room.

"I think I'll stay close to home, work on my research," Carol said. "I might try to find a teaching
position, put down roots. For a few years, at least."

She smiled suddenly, widely. For just a beat,
she almost seemed to glow. "I might buy a little
house somewhere. Plant some flowers."

Leila smiled with her. "That sounds nice."

They paused another moment, Leila not sure
how to say good-bye. The closeness she'd felt

with Carol, since that early morning conversation back on Mars, seemed stronger than ever.

"This is it, I suppose," Carol said finally.

"Yes," Leila said. "I . . . it's been wonderful working with you."

"You too, Leila. I hope I get the opportunity to have you on one of my teams again. Or maybe I'll end up on one of yours."

"Either way, it would be an honor," Leila said.

The two women embraced, promising to keep in touch, and with a final wave, Leila stepped into the transporter. She would go home, put a call in to Professor Bonner, and run herself a long, hot bath, she decided. She wanted to start putting the events of the past few weeks behind her—at least the parts of it that she would have the luxury of forgetting. She would never forget the slight flicker of emotion she had been so sure she had found in the dark eyes of her Vulcan science officer. She realized, as the air began to tingle all around her, that she would always think of him as hers. Perhaps he could never truly belong to her, but he would never belong to anyone else, either.

She watched Carol fade from view, the doctor—her friend—still smiling.

Acknowledgments

This book would not have been possible without the creative input of Britta Dennison, Marco Palmieri, Dr. Joelle Murray, and Paula Block. My few Martian facts came courtesy of the brilliant Robert Zubrin; if they don't read true, it's my fault for messing up the information he shared with me.

As usual, I also thank my friends and family for their ongoing patience and support. And the other *ST* writers for keeping things interesting.

Britta Burdett Dennison would like to thank her family and friends, most of all S. D. Perry for her incredible patience and continued support. Also, thanks to Marco Palmieri and Margaret Clark.

About the Authors

S. D. Perry writes multimedia novelizations in the fantasy/science-fiction/horror realms, for love and money. She lives in Portland, Oregon, with her excellent family, and continues work on an original thriller in her spare time, of which she has very little.

Britta Dennison is a writer living in Portland, Oregon. Previous writing credits include co-authorship of *Star Trek: Deep Space Nine Terok Nor—Night of the Wolves* and *Dawn of the Eagles* with her writing partner, S. D. Perry. She also partnered with Perry on the novelization of *Wonder Woman*. She recently penned a short story for the upcoming anthology *Star Trek: Seven Deadly Sins*.

8